He leaned closer to her and smiled. Willow could see the stubble along his strong jaw, the long lashes that framed his brown eyes—dangerous eyes that held a suggestion of surprising sadness, too.

"I'm not so bad…when you get to know me," he added.

Wrong. She'd known Jack Sullivan for only a few days, but she'd recognized trouble the second she'd looked at him. She took a deep breath. "Getting to know you isn't in our agreement."

He leaned closer. "Not everything has to be by the book…Willow."

His husky whisper of her name shot a shiver down her spine. She had to break free of her attraction to this man.

Dear Reader,

It was a pleasure to set *Wedding Bells at Wandering Creek Ranch* in *my* state of California, where I've lived for the past thirty-five years. I hope to show you another side of the Golden State—not just the bustling Los Angeles area, but the open land and small ranches that are tucked away along the beautiful coastal mountains.

I used this picturesque setting as the backdrop for my story. My heroine grew up with famous movie star parents who valued their privacy and wanted to raise a family outside the prying eyes of Hollywood.

In the story, Willow Kingsley wants to continue the dream of her deceased father, actor Matt Kingsley, who worked with underprivileged children. Her goal is to reopen Kingsley's Kids' Camp at the ranch, but when private investigator Jack Sullivan shows up looking for Willow's brother, it could ruin everything. She has to do something to disguise him, so she turns him into a ranch hand.

I hope you enjoy visiting the Wandering Creek Ranch and the people who live and work there…especially the cowboys.

Thanks for reading,

Patricia Thayer

www.patriciathayer.com

PATRICIA THAYER

Wedding Bells at Wandering Creek Ranch

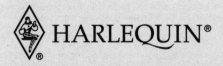

TORONTO • NEW YORK • LONDON
AMSTERDAM • PARIS • SYDNEY • HAMBURG
STOCKHOLM • ATHENS • TOKYO • MILAN • MADRID
PRAGUE • WARSAW • BUDAPEST • AUCKLAND

ISBN-13: 978-0-373-17505-5
ISBN-10:   0-373-17505-1

WEDDING BELLS AT WANDERING CREEK RANCH

First North American Publication 2008.

Western Weddings

In the cowboy's arms...

Imagine a world where men are strong and true
to their word...and where romance always wins
the day! These rugged ranchers may seem
tough on the exterior, but they are about to
meet their match when they meet strong,
loving women to care for them!

If you love gorgeous cowboys and Western settings,
this miniseries is for you!

Look out for more stories in this miniseries,
only from Harlequin Romance®.

Next month in WESTERN WEDDINGS:

JUDY CHRISTENBERRY

Coming Home to the Cattleman

To Mom,
You were always there with your love and support.
Even if I don't say it, I hope you know
how much I appreciate you…. So now am I your favorite?

CHAPTER ONE

SHE LOOKED LIKE every man's fantasy.

Jack Sullivan peered through the grove of oak trees at the woman on horseback. Tall and slender, she rode the large, coal-black stallion with surprising ease. Caught by the breeze, her long wheat-colored hair lifted off her shoulders with each graceful stride. Her slender, jean-clad legs cradled the sides of the horse as they moved through the grassy meadow.

Too bad he wasn't hired to find Willow Kingsley.

Off in the distance, a rocky hillside fringed the seven hundred acres of the Wandering Creek Ranch. Who would have thought an oasis like this existed just thirty miles from Los Angeles? But this ranch was the home of a movie star couple, onetime child star Molly Reynolds and the late western star Matt Kingsley. Their union had produced two children, a son, Dean…and their daughter, Willow.

And Jack was hoping big sister could tell him where to find brother Dean.

A smile appeared on Willow's pretty face as the stallion bobbed its head up and down, protesting her control. She tugged on the reins. "So, you're feeling frisky this morning."

Her voice had a smoky quality, and suddenly, Jack wasn't thinking about business, or about why he'd driven all the way from Seattle to Southern California. Those sultry, whispery tones made him forget that he'd been staking out the ranch for the past twenty-four hours, hoping he'd get lucky and Dean Kingsley would come home to his family. Right now, all Jack could imagine was sister Willow; those long legs, that voice, that…

The stallion whinnied and Jack redirected his attention to the meadow and found Ms. Kingsley was looking at him.

He'd been discovered.

She held her ground and stared back at him. She didn't look happy.

Jack decided since he was on the other side of the electronic fence he wasn't breaking any laws. That wasn't to say as a private investigator he hadn't stretched them a few times. He was used to using any means necessary to locate his suspect.

And he needed to find Kingsley before time ran out…for everyone.

"I would like to talk with you, Ms. Kingsley," he called.

"I don't talk to people who sneak around our property."

"Technically, Ms. Kingsley, I'm not on your property. And I'll leave right away, once you tell me how to find your brother, Dean."

That drew a stronger glare. She just tugged the rein, turned the horse and galloped off.

"Well, you blew that one royally," he chided himself.

He prided himself on handling people with charm and wit. Mike had always said, Jack could con the best of them. An image of Mike, his onetime partner and friend flashed in his head.

"I'm not losing my touch, Mike," he muttered as he hiked back to his SUV. "I'm still going to get my man. It just might take a while longer."

An hour later, after she'd finished brushing down Dakota and putting him into his stall, Willow came out of the barn. She usually enjoyed her morning rides, but today's incident had unnerved her a little.

Since her father's death two years ago, the media had left her and her mother alone, and Willow had hoped they'd forgotten about the Kingsley family entirely. But she supposed the reopening of the summer camp was bound to bring out the press again.

On the way to the house, she stopped short when a black SUV pulled into the circular drive, parked, and the stranger from the pasture got out of his car and started toward the porch.

"Don't take another step," she called out and hurried her pace.

The tall, rangy man turned around and had the nerve to smile. "Hello, Ms. Kingsley. I never got the chance to introduce myself. I'm Jack Sullivan."

Willow ignored the intruder's attempt to charm her. "I don't care who you are, only that you're trespassing."

She glanced toward the foreman's quarters. Where was Trevor? It was his job to keep the gate to the road locked so people couldn't invade their privacy.

"If you leave now, Mr. Sullivan, I won't report to the sheriff that you've been stalking me."

"I'm not stalking you, or anyone." He frowned. "As I tried to explain earlier, I'm looking for Dean Kingsley. My business is with him."

Willow didn't recognize the man who was asking about her brother. He looked to be in his midthirties. He was lean, but a black T-shirt revealed a well-developed chest and broad shoulders, only partially hidden under a rust-colored lightweight jacket. Fitted jeans covered his long legs. She felt a shiver of awareness stir inside her, but quickly shook it off.

"My brother doesn't live here, so please leave. Now. You aren't welcome." She waved toward the road that led back to the Southern California freeway.

"Oh, but, I have been welcomed…by Mrs. Kingsley. She let me in the gate. She's who I'm here to see."

Jack took another step toward the house. He wasn't going anywhere until he at least had a chance to talk to his suspect's mother.

"Willow?" A petite woman appeared in the doorway.

"Mother, it's okay," her daughter said. "This man was just leaving."

So this was Hollywood's famous child star, sweet Molly Reynolds. The young starlet who had once stolen playboy actor Matt Kingsley's heart.

Today, she was in her midfifties, her brown hair styled short around a still-pretty face. She wore a pair of jeans and a Western-cut blouse over her trim figure. She had the same blue eyes as her daughter, but hers held a sadness that affected even a hard-hearted man like himself.

Jack smiled. "Mrs. Kingsley. As I explained over the intercom at the gate, I'm Jack Sullivan, a private investigator." He reached inside his pocket and pulled out a business card. He handed it to her as Willow went to her mother's side. "I tried to tell your daughter…earlier, I'm looking for your son, Dean."

Molly shook her head. "We haven't seen Dean in so long. He's been living and working in Seattle for quite a while now."

"I tried to tell him, Mother, but Mr. Sullivan is insistent." Willow glared at him. "Sorry, we can't help you." She paused. "Now, if you'll excuse us…"

Jack held his ground. Dean Kingsley wasn't getting off just because he came from famous parents and money. No, Jack wasn't about to let that happen again.

"Mrs. Kingsley, do you have an address? Or could you at least tell me the last time your son was home? Does he call you?"

A hint of a smile appeared on the older woman's face. "Dean called last month. He never forgets my birthday."

Did the dutiful son have his family snowed, too? "Other than Seattle or here could you think of another place Dean would go?"

She hesitated. "Is my son in trouble, Mr. Sullivan?"

"I won't lie to you, Mrs. Kingsley. The CEO of Walsh Enterprises, your son's employer, hired me to find Dean. As of right now, we only want to talk with him." Jack hoped his honesty would gain him an ally.

Mother and daughter exchanged a worried look. "I have your card," Molly said, "so I'll call if I hear anything."

Jack didn't know whether to believe her or not, but

he couldn't do much more than smile at them. "I look forward to hearing from you. Please don't hesitate to call that number."

Out of the corners of his eye, Jack caught sight of a man coming from the barn. When he reached the porch, he raised his fingers to his hat in greeting to the ladies. "Is there a problem, Willow?" The man eyed Jack closely.

"It's all right, Trevor," she told him. "Mr. Sullivan is just leaving."

Don't count on it. "I'm not going far…until I find Dean."

The man named Trevor exchanged a knowing look with Kingsley's sister. "I'll make sure he's escorted through the gate."

Jack waited as Willow and her mother went through the door to the house.

"I don't know what your game is, Sullivan," Trevor began, "but you can't just walk onto posted private property."

"I didn't just walk on, I was invited in by Mrs. Kingsley." An easy smile played on Jack's lips as he eyed the man, who was about the same age as himself.

Trevor didn't back down. He straightened to his height of about six feet. "That problem is about to be corrected real soon. And I suggest you don't try to get *invited* back."

The foreman walked Jack to his SUV. He climbed in and started the engine, and backed away from the rustic home of cream-colored stucco, with the stone facade and dark green trim. It hadn't been the mansion he'd expected for Hollywood's royal couple, and pictures of

Willow Kingsley didn't do her justice. Nor had he expected her to be so feisty.

Jack put the car into gear and headed back down the road, passing by the big white barn and corral. The gravel lane was edged with grand oak trees along the white split rail fencing that lined the entrance of the ranch. He glanced in his rearview mirror to see Trevor talking with another man.

Soon a truck was following behind him. No problem, Jack was still going to locate Kingsley. He drove under the archway that read Wandering Creek Ranch.

He was sure they were trying to hide something, as sure as he was of his own name. And he just had to find out what…or who.

After lunch, Willow left her mother in the office working on the vendors list for the summer camp. She went upstairs to make her own call. Although Molly had tried to hide it, she'd been bothered by Mr. Sullivan's inquiry about Dean.

Dean hadn't exactly been the ideal son. Willow never placed all the blame on her brother. It was hard to live up to a movie icon father.

A rush of sadness washed over Willow at the memory of her father. Not just because he'd been a famous movie actor, but because of his presence. Big and strong, he was every woman's ideal man. Even though Matt Kingsley had been portrayed for years as a womanizer, everything changed the second he met Molly Reynolds. Even with the eighteen-year-difference in their ages, they'd stayed faithfully married for thirty-three years… until Matt's death two years ago.

But father and son had had some differences over the years and her brother still felt he'd always be in his father's shadow.

That was the main reason Dean didn't live at the ranch. He went off to work in the Pacific Northwest, hoping it was far enough away that the media would think he wasn't newsworthy anymore.

Willow walked into the bedroom that had been hers since childhood. It had gone through several transformations, most recently in different shades of soft blues. At the desk, she went through her Rolodex to find Dean's number, picked up the phone and made the call to Seattle. After three rings her call was answered by his voice mail.

"Dean. It's Willow. We haven't heard from you in a while. I need to talk to you. Please, give me a call." She paused. "It's important. Love ya, bye."

She hung up and her thoughts returned to Jack Sullivan. She hated the fact that she'd even noticed his dark good looks. It wasn't that she hadn't encountered handsome men before. But Sullivan wasn't your pretty boy Hollywood type. First of all, his nose had been broken, leaving it slightly off center. She doubted he'd ever had his thick sable hair styled. What had drawn her attention was that rough chiseled jaw and those deep-set bedroom eyes.

She suddenly felt her body temperature rise and shook her head to clear any more dangerous thoughts. This man was after her brother.

She sighed. "What have you done now, Dean?"

She used to know everything about her brother. He

hadn't been the rough-and-tumble son Matt Kingsley could relate to. Dean never took to sports, and working the ranch had been more Willow's forte. With Dean it had been computers. Matthew Kingsley's son was a computer nerd.

It had taken Dean years to finally find his calling. So the move to Seattle and the job with Walsh Industries had seemed to be a perfect fit for him. "What happened, Dean? Why is a P.I. looking for you?"

Willow walked to the bed and sat down. Something told her Jack Sullivan was out to destroy her family. No matter what, she wasn't about to let that happen.

Jack groaned as he shifted into what he hoped would be a comfortable position. But there wasn't any, since he was trying to sleep in the front seat of his car.

He hated stakeouts. Nothing to do but wait and think, and struggle against the bad memories that came flooding back.

Memories of one of the few people who'd ever cared about Jack. Mike Gerick. The cop who'd befriended a teenage boy and kept him out of jail. The father figure who'd opened his home to a troubled kid. The man who'd taught him to be a good cop. Mike, who was shot and died in his arms.

What would Mike think about him quitting the force? Jack hoped his friend would give him points for the hard work he'd put into building his P.I. business…now specializing in computer espionage.

So why was Jack sitting out here, sleeping in his car? Because there was evidence that not everything added up at Walsh Enterprises. And it was his job to find out who was responsible.

Jack sat up in his seat and checked his watch. It was after 6:00 a.m. The sun was coming up over the ranch. It was a peaceful scene. To his right in the fenced pasture young foals chased each other in the ankle-high grass. A chestnut stallion whinnied and pranced around, his hoof scraping the ground in impatience at the mare on the other side of the fence.

"I know how you feel, old boy," Jack murmured. His own social life was pretty much nonexistent. Not that it was ever much to begin with. Not with him sitting alone in a car too many nights during stakeouts. Good thing he didn't believe in long-term relationships. Love and romance didn't go with his business. So that pretty much left him out in the cold.

Still, his thoughts turned once again to the pretty Willow. She sure lived up to her name. Tall and slender with those big china-blue eyes. Skin as pale and smooth as a baby's. His fingers flexed with an urgency to touch her that surprised him.

Suddenly there was a rap against his window and he jumped. He jerked around to discover the woman in his daydream standing next to his car.

He turned the key and hit the button to lower the glass. "Is there a problem, Ms. Kingsley?"

"You know darn well there's a problem, Mr. Sullivan. What are you doing here?"

"I'm waiting…" He gave her the once-over. This morning, she had on worn jeans and a fitted blue shirt that brought out the color of her eyes. "And enjoying the scenery." He folded his arms over his chest and tried out an intimidating glare.

She ignored it. "You're trespassing." She peered into the interior of his car. Jack knew she was seeing the well-known coffee company's cups that littered the floor, and last night's dinner wrappers wadded up on the passenger seat. A total mess, and he didn't look much better.

"I beg to differ, Ms. Kingsley, I'm not on your property."

She huffed and marched back to the truck that was parked behind his SUV. Boy, he sure was slipping. He hadn't even heard her drive up. Mike would rag on him for the rookie mistake. Jack expected Willow to drive off, but she didn't, instead she made a call on her cell phone.

When she was finished, she got out of her vehicle and came back to him. "For your information, Mr. Sullivan, I called the sheriff. Perhaps you'd rather leave now, before there's trouble…."

He wanted to show her his kind of trouble all right. She reminded him of Mary Ellen McGowan in fifth grade, who'd gotten pleasure from tattling on him. He shook his head. "You can't dictate where I park."

"I can if you're stalking me."

"Get over yourself Ms. Hollywood," he growled. "Or how about telling me where your brother is hiding out."

Her nostrils flared. "My brother isn't hiding anywhere. So just leave."

She was either the best liar, or she didn't have a clue. "No, I'll wait for the deputy."

She made that superior huffing sound again and began to pace. "Why are you so persistent?" She

stopped and glared at him. "We already told you everything we know."

"I'm persistent because it's important I find your
brother…and soon. It's my job."

Her gaze locked with his, and he felt a shudder rush
through him. Damn. She was a pretty package. Luckily,
he was immune to her type.

"Could you at least tell me who wants to see Dean
so badly?"

"Will you tell me if you've been in touch with him
in the past week?"

"No, I haven't been in touch with Dean."

Jack frowned.

"It's true," she stressed. "Right after you left yesterday, I called his cell phone, but I only got his voice mail.
Now, who's looking for him?"

"I'm not at liberty to say at this time."

She folded her arms over her breasts and glared.

Before Jack could say anything more, the sheriff's
patrol car pulled up.

"Now, you're in trouble," Willow said and marched
over to the deputy who had just climbed out of the car.
She motioned with her hands as she explained her take
on the situation. Like the ranch foreman, the young
deputy appeared enamored by Willow Kingsley, too.

He approached Jack's car. "Sir, would you please
step out of the vehicle?"

"Sure, Officer." Jack opened the door and stood by
the car.

"May I see some ID?"

"It's in my pocket." He hesitated, then with the

deputy's nod, he pulled out his badge holder and flipped it open to show his ID and driver's license from the state of Washington.

"I'm going to run this. Stay here."

"Fine." Jack leaned against the car door and folded his arms across his chest. "I'm not going anywhere, Willow, so get used to it. Not until I speak to Dean. Right away if possible."

Just then the deputy returned. "Okay, no prior warrants." He handed back Jack's license.

She dug her fists into her hips. "That's it, Shawn?"

"Sorry, Willow." He glanced at Jack. "He's not on private property. So he's free to be here."

"He can't stay parked out there," Willow protested as she walked back and forth in front of the kitchen's French doors the next morning. Her mother and Trevor were seated at the table for breakfast. Willow had no appetite after her confrontation with the P.I.

"Nothing we can do about it," Trevor offered as he glanced up at Regina Vargas. The young housekeeper set a plate of eggs and bacon in front of him. He smiled and thanked her, and his gaze lingered on the pretty, dark-haired Gina as she walked back to the stove.

He sobered and glanced back at Willow. "We'll need to find Dean so he can explain what's going on."

"I called him." Willow shook her head. "And I got his voice mail. Besides, that's not going to stop Jack Sullivan right now. What will happen if the media gets wind that a P.I. is snooping around? We've more to think about than the tabloids. What about the donations for

Kingsley's Kids, and the summer camp opening in a few weeks?" Years ago her father started a charity to help disadvantaged kids. It was his way of dealing with the demons of his own dismal childhood.

Molly Kingsley stood. "It's going to be all right, Willow. I'm sure Dean will straighten this all out when he calls."

Willow smiled. That was her mom, the eternal optimist.

"Besides," Molly continued. "We've nearly reached our sponsorship goal for the camp."

True, but Willow knew how easily a charity could lose funding because of bad press. Ever since Matt Kingsley's death, she and her mother had had some difficultly rebuilding financial aid for the project.

Willow had promised her father she would keep the camp going. It was also close to her mother's heart, just what Molly needed to fill her time. And with a lot of hard work, it was finally coming true. This was the first time in two years the Kingsley's Kids Camp was able to open their doors again.

She couldn't let Jack Sullivan distract her from her goal.

"If word gets around of a P.I. looking for Dean, it could ruin everything."

Her mother stared through the glass toward the road where the SUV was parked. "Then we need to disguise Mr. Sullivan." She turned and looked at her daughter, then at Trevor. "So he's not as noticeable."

"I'd like to hide him out back in the manure pile," Trevor said, giving up on his breakfast.

Molly smiled brightly. "Close, but why not put him

to work while he's hanging around waiting for Dean? I mean, you can use some help, right, Trevor?"

Willow blinked. "Sure, but Sullivan doesn't look the type who knows much about the workings of a ranch."

"He looked pretty buff to me." Molly grinned mischievously. "He can lift and tote."

Willow blinked. "Mother, surely you can't be thinking of hiring him? Of bringing him onto the property?"

"It's a lot better than having him parked out there drawing attention."

"What makes you think he'll agree to do it?" Willow asked.

"Because he wants to find Dean," Molly said. "And I want to learn more about what kind of trouble my son is in."

Willow didn't want any stranger hanging around, but she liked it even less that this particular man was literally camped on their doorstep. "First, I'll have Jack Sullivan checked out. Then, and only then, will I consider going along with this crazy idea."

"It isn't crazy if it protects our family," her mother said.

Willow had grown up in the spotlight. She wasn't sure anything could protect them.

CHAPTER TWO

"IT NEVER RAINS in Southern California," Jack murmured as he squinted through the water-sheeted windshield. "Not in the summertime, anyway. Yeah, right." It had been drizzling most of the night and half the day.

As a Seattle native, he should be used to wet weather, but he hated the rain. He leaned back in the seat, wishing this job was over. What he'd hoped would be a quick trip was now dragging out. Maybe he should just cut his losses and try another lead.

Problem was, there were no other leads. He also knew he needed to be less conspicuous. Parking on the edge of the ranch property wasn't going to surprise the suspect.

Jack rubbed his hand over his face. Last night he'd gotten a room at a motel along the highway, showered and ate some dinner, then made the call to Stan Walsh.

The CEO was impatient. He wanted Kingsley in the worst way. To top it off, it turned out that Dean was romantically involved with the boss's daughter, Heather. It seemed he'd left her high and dry, too, when he took off. The only thing Kingsley had in his favor was that Walsh didn't want the stockholders to learn of the…situation, yet. That gave Jack a few weeks to find the man so they could handle the problem quietly…and privately.

Jack tensed. Dean Kingsley couldn't go unpunished for what he'd done. But in real life guilty men often were set free, especially when they had affluent families to pay for high-powered lawyers to get them off.

Jack knew all too well how that played out, and how the legal system didn't always work for the average person. It hadn't for Mike…. His best friend didn't get justice. His killer walked away a free man.

Jack's cell phone rang and pulled him out of his reverie. He flipped it open. "Sullivan, here."

"Mr. Sullivan. It's Willow Kingsley."

He sat up straighter. "Hello, Ms. Kingsley. Have you heard from your brother?"

"No, we haven't, but my mother and I would like to talk with you. Could you come up to the house…for dinner? We have a business proposition for you."

Her husky voice sent a heated tremor through his body. Business. Remember, she said business. "What time?"

"Six o'clock."

"I'll see you then." He slapped the phone closed. Things were starting to look up.

After a quick trip back to the motel to shave and change into a fresh shirt, Jack managed to make it to the house in the allotted time.

Willow answered the door. Tonight she wore a long blue skirt made out of a gauzy material and a cream-colored peasant-style blouse. She looked soft and feminine. Made him glad he'd managed to freshen up.

Silently she motioned him inside. He stepped across the threshold and into the great room. A stone fireplace took up most of the far wall. Below an open-beamed ceiling was a winding staircase and carved wood railing that exposed the entire length of the second floor. Hardwood planks ran throughout the large area, partly covered by braided rugs and overstuffed, well-used leather furniture.

He glanced at Willow in time to catch a knowing look in those incredible eyes.

"Surprised, Mr. Sullivan?"

"At what?"

"That my family doesn't live in a Louis the Fourteenth style mansion."

He raised an eyebrow. "You had a home in Beverly Hills."

"When my father worked in the business," she said. "But this was where he wanted to be. Away from all the attention, luxury and the press." Her stare dared him to comment.

He didn't.

"Our one consolation was that Dad got to spend his last days here," she told him. "In the home that he loved." Tears laced her voice and he hated that it affected him.

"I'm truly sorry for your loss. I'm sure your father found comfort here with his loved ones around." It was obvious Willow was close to her family. "Was Dean here then?"

She sighed. "Mr. Sullivan…"

"Don't you think this would be easier if we were on a first name basis? I'm Jack. May I call you Willow?"

Willow hated that the man could be so rude one minute, then the next, flash a smile and expect her to just melt. Well, she'd made that mistake before. Never again.

But she nodded. "All right then, Jack."

"Okay, Willow, why don't you tell me about this proposition you have."

"It was my mother's idea," she said. "I'll let her explain." She led him through the dining room, past a long table that could seat a dozen people and into a big country kitchen.

The room had honey maple cabinets and shiny black granite countertops. He caught a whiff of something spicy cooking. His stomach growled, reminding him he'd had a packet of peanut butter crackers for lunch.

Off in a corner in front of French doors, Molly Reynolds and the foreman stood at the table. Another young woman in jeans and white blouse was setting the table.

"You've met my mother."

"Hello, Mrs. Kingsley."

She smiled. "Mr. Sullivan."

"Please call me, Jack."

The pretty woman returned his smile. "And everyone calls me Molly."

The expression on Willow's face told him she didn't like the familiarity. He turned his attention to the foreman.

The man eyed him closely. "Sullivan. I'm Trevor Adams, foreman."

So, Trevor Adams wasn't going to be his friend. He saw Jack as too much of a threat. "Adams," Jack said.

"And this is Gina Vargas," Willow added as the young

Hispanic woman looked up from her task. "She keeps the house in order and she's the best cook around."

"Gina, I'm looking forward to the meal. It smells great."

"Thank you," she said shyly. "Here's your place."

"I hope you don't mind eating in the kitchen," Molly said.

He grinned. "I'm a kitchen kind of guy. And being a bachelor I'm looking forward to a home-cooked meal." He waited until the women took their places, then he sat down.

Gina set a tall glass of iced tea at his place. Then she returned with a large casserole filled with bubbling chicken enchiladas. She added bowls of beans, rice and a stack of tortillas.

It began to rain again, and as it sheeted down on the brick patio outside, Molly dished out generous portions of food and handed the first to Jack, then did the same for the others. He added his own beans and rice, then dug in.

There was some polite conversation about the weather and then came the questions.

"How long have you been in business for yourself, Jack?" Molly asked.

"About five years." He took a drink of sweet tea. "But you already know that…and probably a lot more." All they'd had to do was read his ad in the Seattle area Yellow Pages, or check his Web site.

Molly gave him an innocent smile. "I thought it was interesting that you were on the Seattle Police Force for three years."

"You've been a busy lady, Molly."

"If I've learned anything from growing up in Hollywood, it's not to trust many people. Not to take them at face value, anyway. But I can't take all the credit. My daughter is very thorough." Her intent gaze held his. "Your ad also states you specialize in white-collar investigations. Does that mean you're after Dean for a crime?"

"I'm not at liberty to discuss the particulars of the case. You know your son better than I do. You tell me."

Willow glared at him. "Dean would never steal…."

Willow braced herself for more questions from the man. Instead Jack just studied her, which was even more disconcerting.

"I never said he stole anything," he finally said. "The reason I'm looking for him…is just to talk with him." Jack spoke in between bites. "It's not an unfair request, especially since he hasn't been to work in the past week."

"So it's his boss from Walsh Enterprises that hired you?"

He took another drink of his tea, ignoring her question. "Since Dean hasn't been seen at his apartment, logical reasoning would be to think he came to visit his family…especially if he needs help."

Willow didn't know what to say. She couldn't believe that her brother would do anything unethical…certainly not steal money. And she certainly didn't want to give Jack any more information about the family. It was important that he not learn that Matt Kingsley had cut off the purse strings to his son years ago. Every dime of her father's estate was tied up in a trust until after Molly'd passed on.

Trevor dropped his fork on his plate. "So you're

going to hang out here and bushwhack Dean when or if he shows up."

Jack ignored Adams and turned his attention to Willow and Molly. "I'm not playing any games with your family. I'm trying to help. It is imperative that Dean clears something up before it becomes a legal matter."

"Then let's help each other," Molly offered. "We want to keep our lives private, and escape media notice. Having you parked on the edge of the ranch will draw attention."

"I'm not leaving…"

Molly raised her hand. "We know. So we're offering you access to our property, and our word that we'll let you know if Dean contacts us."

Jack's eyes narrowed.

"But only if you promise not to tell anyone you're a private investigator, and pretend that you work here…as a ranch hand."

He wasn't sure if Molly Kingsley was kidding or not. "You want me to play cowboy?"

"Maybe. We won't ask you to bust any wild horses," Willow said. "But there are other things you can do around the ranch. And we can teach you a few things so you can get by." She turned to her mother. "A good cover might be that he's a friend of Dean's."

Molly nodded. "I do have one concern. Can you handle about three dozen rowdy kids? Because in a little over a week, we're reopening our annual summer camp."

"By then I'll be out of here."

"One would hope," Willow said.

Jack couldn't help but smile. "Okay, I'll do it. I mean how hard can it be?"

* * *

Jack had held back one bit of information. He actually had spent some time on a working ranch. After he'd been labeled a troubled kid, his mother was more than happy to get rid of her twelve-year-old son for a couple of months. He hated leaving his friends in town to go to a police sponsored summer camp, but in the end he'd enjoyed his time in the country. Back then, he'd considered himself such a badass he wouldn't give anyone the satisfaction of knowing he liked anything.

Until Mike got a hold of him. The tough cop refused to put up with a teenager's foul mouth and bad attitude. Damn. If Mike could see him now. "What goes around comes around," he'd told Jack so many times.

An hour after dinner, carrying his duffel bag, Jack followed Trevor into the bunkhouse. They entered into a large main room with rough-cedar walls divided up into different areas. In the kitchen area three long tables took up the space.

Along one wall was a huge sofa and two recliners. Two men occupied chairs facing a large television tuned to a baseball game.

"Ted and Larry," Trevor began. "This is Jack Sullivan. He just hired on and will be bunking here with you."

Both men greeted him with a wave as Trevor continued the tour, down the hall to the first of three smaller rooms. Here there were four bunks, two already made up. Jack tossed his things on a vacant one next to the window.

"The bathroom is at the end of the hall, bed linens

and towels are in the cupboard. Breakfast is at six after the morning chores are finished."

Jack could see Adams enjoyed playing boss. "When do we get up?"

"About five. The stock gets fed first."

Jack grinned. "Not a problem. I can handle that."

The foreman glared at him. "Just follow the rules, Sullivan, and we'll get along fine."

"Don't worry, Adams, I'll do my part."

Trevor pushed his hat back on his head. "We'll see." He turned to leave when Willow appeared in the doorway. "Willow, is there a problem?"

"No, I came to talk to Jack."

Trevor studied her for a moment, then shrugged and left them alone.

She glanced around the room, then turned to Jack. "As you can see the accommodations are pretty basic…. Not much privacy, either."

He'd lived in worse. "It beats sleeping in my car." He caught a hint of a smile from her as he sat down on the single-sized mattress. "And the bunk is comfortable."

"My mother had them all replaced just recently." She moved farther into the room carrying a canvas tote bag. "Of course you aren't going to get a lot of sleep. And tomorrow will be rough so I thought you might need these." From the bag she pulled a pair of black boots. They were well-worn, but he could tell they were top-of-the-line. "What's your size?" she asked.

"Twelve."

"Then these should fit you."

He wasn't sure he should take them. Why was she suddenly being so nice?

She glanced down at his black leather athletic shoes. "We can't pull this off if you don't at least look the part."

He reached for them and kicked off his shoes. He was about to slip one on when he saw the initials MK inside. "These were you father's."

She nodded.

He felt like a heel. "I know you don't want me here, Willow."

She glanced away. "I told you before we value our privacy."

"And I have a job to do."

"You don't have any proof that Dean is guilty of… whatever."

"That's the reason I'm here. To talk to him."

After a moment she sighed and said, "You're wasting your time. Dean won't come here. The ranch wasn't his favorite place."

Jack studied her. Before coming to California, he'd done extensive research on the Kingsley family. He knew all about the twenty-nine-year-old Willow's well-publicized engagement and breakup, and the unauthorized private pictures her ex-fiancé sold to the tabloids. He didn't blame her for being leery of strangers.

"I give you my word, Willow. I'll do my best to keep the matter with Dean private…but that's up to your brother."

"Just remember we're giving you this opportunity so the press won't be involved."

"Believe me, my client doesn't want to publicize this situation any more than you do."

She watched him with those intriguing blue eyes,

but her firm jawline showed her determination, her refusal to back down. He knew she'd protect her family no matter what.

Who protected her?

Jack's job was to find people's vulnerability. Although Willow Kingsley hid hers well, he'd seen that, too. He'd caught glimpses of her softness, definitely her beauty. Yes, definitely, her beauty wasn't lost on him. His chest tightened as his body began to stir with awareness.

She finally broke the spell and glanced down at the boots. "You better see if those fit."

"Right." Jack busied himself tugging on the boots, then stood to check the fit. The soft leather felt good. "Not bad," he announced with a smile.

She nodded. "Be sure to wear a long-sleeved shirt and there are extra hats on the rack in the barn. There should be one that fits you." She glanced around the room again. "If there's anything else you need, Trevor should be able to get it for you." She paused. "Good night…Jack."

She turned to leave and he found himself trying to find a way to stop her. "Will I see you tomorrow?"

Willow paused at the room's entrance, her full lips parted, hesitating, then she said, "I usually ride most mornings, but you already know that."

He nodded, unable to forget how graceful she was on horseback. "Then I'll look for you."

"I'm not sure that's a good idea."

He frowned. "Wait a minute. I thought we were going to come up with a story that I'm a friend of your brother's. That way we can talk to each other, and it will also explain my inexperience with horses."

"You're right. I just don't want people to think…" Her pretty face reddened.

"That there's something between us," he finished for her, hating that the idea so obviously bothered her.

She nodded. This time she didn't hide her sadness. "It's been rough since Dad's death. Mother has only now been willing to go public with the reopening of the camp. It was important to her—to us that we keep the camp going."

Jack walked to her. The boots added another inch or so to his six-foot-two height. Her gaze widened as he approached and he wondered where the strong, brassy woman who tried to chase him away had gone. He caught an unguarded glint in her eyes, a hesitant tone in her voice. He knew she didn't let people see this side often. It made a man feel protective…almost.

"So being Matt Kingsley's good daughter," he said, "you took charge and got things going again."

Willow stiffened, and her eyes flashed. "That's the thing, Jack. I wasn't always the good daughter."

Willow hated that she was actually looking for the man when she walked into the barn early the next morning. Jack Sullivan was trouble. As much as she wanted to believe him, she wasn't sure he was here to help her brother.

Trust didn't come easy for her, especially with men.

All she'd ever wanted was to find a love like her parents had. Married for thirty years was a rare thing in Hollywood, or anywhere. She could still see the loving look in her father's eyes whenever her mother walked into a room.

For years, whenever Matt Kingsley went on location for a movie the media had tried to stir up rumors of an illicit romance. But her parents' love had survived whatever the tabloid press threw at them.

And Willow had thought she'd found a man who emulated her father, Scott Richfield. Instead, she got someone who wanted the limelight that came along with her famous family…but not her. Only her father's death had made her realize what kind of man Scott was. At her lowest point he'd hadn't been there for her and in the end he'd betrayed her. And after all this time, it still stung.

Willow walked through the barn doors, and down the aisle to Dakota's stall. "Good morning, old guy," she crooned to the raven-black quarter horse that had been her father's faithful companion.

The horse tossed his head, then came to the gate for some attention. She rubbed his forehead. "You want to go for a run this morning?"

He whinnied in response, and she went to the end of the barn to the tack room. That's where she found Jack. She gasped. "Sorry, I didn't expect anyone to be in here."

Jack looked up from cleaning a saddle with a chamois cloth. "Trevor wants all the tack cleaned and oiled."

That was true, but she sympathized with his being stuck here all day in the tiny room. "So how did the morning go with everyone?"

He shrugged. "Not bad. I met the other ranch hands at breakfast, and Larry took me out to help feed the horses. After that Trevor handed me this assignment."

Okay, she might have to talk with Trevor. She went

to the wall and took down a bridle, then reached for her saddle.

"How about a reprieve?" Jack asked as he stood and came to help her.

She paused. "I thought you agreed to this."

"I agreed to play the part of a ranch hand, not be locked away in a room all day."

Willow turned to the man who was dressed in Levi's and a long-sleeved denim shirt. She noticed he had on the boots she'd given him. He looked as though he belonged here. But he didn't and she had to remember that.

"Since you don't know much else…" She began to lift her saddle, but he stepped in.

"I have a confession to make." He took the saddle from the stand, then followed her out of the room and back to Dakota's stall. "When I was twelve, I spent a summer on a ranch."

"What else have you neglected to tell us, Mr. Sullivan?"

He placed the saddle on the bench and his dark eyes locked with hers. "That's pretty much it."

She nodded. "Then I guess we both can get to work."

He cocked his thumb toward the tack room. "Come on, Willow, you can't send me back in there."

"It's not my call," she told him. "Trevor probably had a good reason for putting you to work there."

"You're the boss. You make the rules."

She folded her arms over her chest. "Maybe I should just ask what job you'd like."

He braced his shoulder against the post and grinned. "Okay, I'd like to go riding with you."

She couldn't hide her surprise. "You're kidding, right?"

He just kept on smiling. "What can I say? I like playing cowboy."

"Riding a horse can be dangerous. You need to know what you're doing."

"It'll come back to me."

She opened the stall door. "I can't risk it."

"Can't or won't?" he asked. "I've done what your mother asked. Aren't all the other hands going to wonder why I'm stuck in the tack room? At least let me prove that I can handle a horse."

Willow hated to admit it, but he was right. He was trying to cooperate. Her problem was she didn't want him here at all.

She latched the stall. "Follow me," she told him and marched down the aisle. She stopped three stalls away where a gray gelding was housed. "This is Cisco. He's pretty gentle." She patted the animal's forehead. "He'll be your mount."

"You're serious?" He reached out and stroked the horse's neck, impressing her with his ease around the animal. "You're going to let me ride."

"Only if you can tack up your own horse. Do you think you can?"

He grinned again and her pulse soared.

"If it will get me out of the barn, I'm willing to give it a damn good try."

"Okay, but don't think you're going to get out of working. All the hands carry their weight."

"Yes, ma'am," he said with another of his disturbing grins.

Willow didn't want to find him disturbing. "Good,

because the tack will be waiting for you when you get back."

She turned and walked away, hearing him chuckle behind her. The sound made her smile, too.

But inside, Willow knew that this man was a threat to her and her family. All the time he was here he would be watching them. She had to be vigilant. Jack Sullivan was a man with a mission. He would throw her brother to the wolves if need be.

Twenty minutes later Jack grabbed a straw cowboy hat off a peg and led a saddled Cisco out of the barn. So far so good, he thought. He was enjoying himself. Something he hadn't done in a long time.

He found Willow in the corral. She was bending over, checking her horse's front hoof. He couldn't help but notice how nicely her jeans fit over her rounded bottom and legs.

He quickly shook away the direction of his thoughts. He needed to keep his focus on the job. That made Willow Kingsley off-limits.

Willow released the horse's leg and straightened. "Well, that didn't take too long." She walked around Cisco, checking how well Jack had done saddling the animal.

She took hold of the stirrup and tossed it over the saddle to check the cinch. Pushing on the horse's side, she tested to see if the strap was tight enough. It was.

She eyed him. "So, you learned Cisco's trick."

He adjusted his hat. "You mean when he holds his breath until you think the cinch is tight, then lets it's out when you try to mount and your saddle slips? Yeah,

I did. He isn't the only horse who pulls that. So do I pass the test?"

"Let's see how you handle him."

Jack glanced around and found they had an audience. A few of the ranch hands had gathered to watch. Then Trevor came out of the barn and walked toward them. "Hey, Sullivan. I thought I left you cleaning tack."

Willow stepped forward. "I'm the one who relieved Jack of the job."

The foreman frowned. "Willow, do you think this is a good idea?"

"What's so unusual about a ranch hand riding?" Willow asked. "Seems Jack already knows how."

Adams looked angry. "You don't say," he said through clenched teeth.

Jack really didn't want to make an enemy of the man, but he wasn't about to back down, either. "It was a long time ago, so Willow offered to help me with a refresher lesson."

The foreman turned back to Willow. "I can assign Larry to him."

She shook her head. "They all have work to do today. And so do you. I thought you were going to the Carson place to check on the extra saddle horses." She looked at Jack. "We have neighbors who are willing to loan us some mounts for the camp. We want to be sure we have enough horses for all the kids."

"That's a lot of animals to feed and care for."

"And it's the reason we can't have any distractions," Trevor told him. "Everything needs to be in place before the kids arrive at the end of next week."

Willow stepped in between the two men. "Then you better get going, Trevor. And be sure to thank Mimi Carson for me."

"Will do," Trevor said, tossing another warning glare at Jack before he stalked off.

"He's very protective of you," Jack said.

Willow smiled. "I know. I used to be annoyed by it, but there have been times…that I've been grateful."

"Like when I showed up."

She tipped back her cowboy hat and exposed her face to the warm sun. "Maybe. If you'd done any research, you'd know that Trevor Adams is family. His father, Sligh Adams, was my dad's stunt double and best friend. Trevor and I practically grew up together. He's like a brother."

"Are you sure Adams thinks of you as his sister?" Jack asked. And would the man's loyalties go so far as to hide Dean? he added silently.

Her smile disappeared. "That's an old tabloid story, Mr. Sullivan. So if you're trying to dig up dirt—"

"No," he interrupted her. "I apologize, I have no right to speculate on your private life."

"That's right, you don't. You know nothing about who I am, or who any of the Kingsleys are."

Seeing the hurt in her eyes, he wished for once he'd kept his mouth shut.

"Here's another rule," she began. "From now on, my personal life is off-limits…unless it pertains to finding Dean. If you can't agree to that, our deal is off."

She didn't leave him much choice. He nodded. "I

agree. Your personal life is off-limits." He took a step closer. "But all bets are off if I discover you're keeping information about Dean's whereabouts from me."

CHAPTER THREE

WILLOW HATED THE FACT that Jack could handle a horse so well. But no doubt the man was good at a lot of things.

"You never told me how a city kid ended up on a ranch," she asked.

He gave her a sideways glance, and mostly kept his eye on what he was doing as they rode along the trail. "I thought we weren't going to get personal."

"I didn't know asking you how you learned to ride was all that personal," she said.

"Truth is, I'd gotten into some trouble in my youth. I was running around with some wild kids and we got caught shoplifting. I was offered camp for the summer."

She raised an eyebrow. "So you were a budding juvenile delinquent."

"You could say that. My mother was ready to give up on me."

"What about your father?"

"Wasn't in the picture…hadn't been for a long time."

"I'm sorry."

"Not a big deal. I survived just fine."

Willow wondered about that. She'd always taken her

caring parents for granted. She also knew how much she missed her father now. How could a young boy cope with that kind of void in his life?

"Seems to me a child needs both parents," she said.

His expression was stony. "Not all of us had a fairy-tale life."

Her back straightened. "I really get tired of hearing that. You know appearances can be deceiving." She kicked Dakota's sides and shot off in a run. She needed time alone, time not filled with another man judging her.

Jack wanted to ride after her, but he'd never catch up, nor would she be happy if he tried. They both had probed a little too deep. He usually didn't talk about his past. It was nobody's business. He couldn't change it, so no use crying about it. That was what Mike always told him when he'd start feeling sorry for himself. He missed his partner's wisdom, their talks.

Jack watched Willow as she circled the meadow, letting Dakota run at will. No doubt she could handle the large stallion. He liked that about her. Her strength. She would use it to defend her family, too.

He suspected Dean hadn't inherited the same trait. Was he guilty of a crime? Why would Matt Kingsley's son have to steal? The family had to be loaded, or was it just a game to the computer wizard?

"If that's so, Dean, old boy, your family will be the ones who get hurt," he murmured.

Willow's yellow hair fanned out as she leaned low over the horse's neck. The stallion picked up speed as it and its rider did one more pass, then finally slowed and trotted up next to him.

"That was quite a show," he said.

She patted the horse's sweaty neck and tried to catch her breath. "Dakota loves to run. Even at eighteen he hasn't slowed down."

They walked together for a minute. Jack glanced around the seemingly endless acres of green meadow, skirted by the mountain range and he shifted in the saddle. Cisco made him look good, and responded readily to the slightest command. "This is quite a backyard you have here."

Willow sighed. "I know. It's perfect. And developers think so, too."

"I expect the land is pretty valuable."

"Well, seven hundred acres is probably too much for just Mom and me."

The horses moved with a slow, easy rhythm. "But not with the kid's camp."

She shrugged. "It's only open a few weeks out of the summer. I suppose we should be doing much more than just that, but…"

"What about running cattle?"

"We used to have a small herd at one time. Back when Dad filmed westerns here." She pointed off toward the mountains. "In fact, the movie set still exists out there."

"You're kidding. You actually have your own western town with a jail and a saloon?"

"And a one-room school house and a church." Her smile faded. "Then when my father got sick, he couldn't work…. So he concentrated on the camp."

"That has to be an expensive undertaking."

"Yes, but Dad was good at getting financial sponsors."

"Enough to keep it going now?"

She shot him a sideways glance. "I don't like where this is leading."

"It's not leading anywhere. It's just conversation."

She didn't seem to accept his explanation. "Are you accusing my brother of stealing—"

He raised a hand. "I'm not accusing him of anything. I was just curious as to how you keep the camp going?"

"For one thing, the ranch is ours free and clear. And Mother and I work hard to get funding to reopen the camp."

"Sounds like a big undertaking."

"But well worth it." She seemed to relax and smile. Jack had trouble concentrating on business. Willow nodded toward Cisco.

"How are you feeling? Tired?"

Every one of Jack's muscles ached but he wasn't about to share that with her. "Not bad."

"Good." She looked ahead toward a group of trees. "I have something to show you if you can keep up."

He caught a glimmer of humor in her eyes. "Is that a challenge?"

"Maybe," she called as she kicked Dakota into a run.

When Jack spurred Cisco, the horse responded and took off after her.

With Willow in the lead, they made it to the edge of what looked exactly like the main street of an old western town.

"Welcome to Liberty." Willow climbed down from Dakota and walked the animal to the hitching post, then went to the side of the building, turned on a spigot and water came out the end of the hose. She dragged it out to the street and began to fill a nearby trough.

Jack swung his leg over Cisco's back, feeling every muscle in his body cry for mercy.

"You still okay?" Willow asked.

"Yeah, I'm fine." He looked around. He'd never been much of a movie buff, but even he remembered the famous television miniseries about an older sheriff hired to tame a lawless town. Of course, it had starred Matt Kingsley.

Willow brought the hose to her lips and took a long drink, then handed it to Jack. "Drink up. It's spring water."

"None of that fancy bottled water for you, huh?"

She smiled again. "Nothing tastes better than this."

He drank deep. She was right. "Very good."

They left the horses at the trough and headed down the main street. "I feel like I should be wearing a gun and spurs." He tilted his hat back and looked at the two story weathered structures. "Are the buildings finished inside, too?"

"Most of them are because they filmed inside as well as outside."

Willow realized she was proud and happy to show Jack around. The first stop, the saloon, where she opened a glass-paneled door to reveal a pair of swinging bar doors. "The strong Santa Ana winds that blow during the winter here have probably left a coat of dust on everything."

Once Willow was inside wonderful memories flooded back. She was just out of college, old enough to work on the production with her dad.

She crossed the planked floors, dusted now with sandy soil, to the long oak bar, with it's mirrored backsplash and shelves filled with bottles. Several round tables were scattered around the room, and an upright piano rested against the far wall. A staircase led to the second floor.

"So what's upstairs?" Jack asked.

They both looked to the door beyond the open railing. "There's about four rooms." She shrugged. "For the saloon girls…and their customers."

"Ah, so it was a full-service saloon."

She bit her bottom lip. "Of course."

Willow turned and walked out. Jack followed and they continued down the wooden sidewalk past the general store to the jail. In the front half there was a desk, and in back a prison cell containing only a narrow bunk draped with an army-green blanket.

Jack sat down to sample the lumpy mattress. "Not very grand accommodations."

"Well, if you break the law in Liberty, you don't deserve much." Willow stood at the entrance, surprised at Jack's almost boyish enthusiasm. "My dad was the town's sheriff. And he always caught the bad guys. All of them," she stressed.

His dark gaze caught hers and seemed to pin her there. "Do you think of me as the bad guy?"

She wanted to believe he was on their side, just as she prayed Dean wasn't in any bad trouble. "Maybe."

He stood and came toward her. "I'm just doing my job, Willow."

Even though her heart pounded erratically, she refused to back away. "At whose expense?"

He shrugged. "If your brother will talk with me, and

I'm satisfied with his answers, I'll leave and never bother you again."

He leaned closer to her and smiled. She could see the beard stubble along his strong jaw, the long lashes that framed his brown eyes. Dangerous eyes that held a suggestion of surprising sadness, too.

"I'm not so bad…when you get to know me," he added.

Wrong. She'd known Jack Sullivan for only a few days but she'd recognized trouble the second she looked at him. She took a deep breath. "Getting to know you isn't in our agreement."

He leaned closer. "Not everything has to be by the book…Willow."

His husky whisper of her name shot a shiver down her spine. She had to break free of her attraction to this man. "We should get back to the ranch."

Willow took a step backward, accidentally bumping into the cell door, causing it to shut. Then as if everything were happening in slow motion, the key on the outside of the cell fell from the lock, hit the floor and bounced away. Out of their reach.

"Oh, no." She tried to force the cell door open, but it wouldn't budge. "We're locked in."

Jack rattled the door, then frowned at her. "Okay, the joke's over, where's the release?"

Did he think she wanted to be in here with him? "How should I know?"

Jack examined the bars. "My God, these are real iron."

"I know. Dad liked everything being authentic."

"I can't believe that he wouldn't fix it so the door didn't lock."

Jack checked where the wall and bars met. Rusty pins held the rails in place. Taking out his Swiss Army knife, he chose the screwdriver attachment and inserted it under the bolt head. He struggled to get leverage, but the pin didn't move.

Willow came up behind him. "Is it coming out?"

He worked hard to ignore her clean citrus scent, the husky quality of her voice. But when her breasts brushed against his back his entire body went on alert.

Damn. He had to get out of there. With a grunt he put all his weight into the job, and the screwdriver head broke off. He turned and looked into her blue eyes. "I guess that answers your question." He tossed the knife on the bunk in frustration.

"We can't stay here," she told him. "We don't even have any water…and the horses."

"They have water," he reminded her, but that didn't help the two of them. "Does anyone know where you were going?"

She shook her head. "I wasn't planning on coming here."

"Well, it's time we let someone know." He pulled out his cell phone from his jeans pocket, but saw that it signaled no reception. "Damn, my phone isn't working here. What about yours?"

"It's in my saddlebag." Willow sank down on the bunk. "We'll just have to wait until someone comes looking for us."

Great. And Jack knew just who that would be. All he needed was for Trevor to charge in and rescue them.

He'd never live it down. He eyed the key again. There had to be a way to get to it, something to hook it with.

He reached out to Willow. "Let me have your belt."

Without hesitation she unbuckled the simple black belt from her small waist and gave it to him. "You think this will work?"

"I hope so, but while I'm trying, start thinking up another idea." He turned his attention to the task of buckling his belt with hers. When he finished he reached through the bars, working to get the looped belt around the key.

Ten minutes later, Jack finally gave up. Sitting on the floor, he bent up his knees and looked at her on the bunk. "Any suggestions?"

"No." With a sigh, Willow leaned against the wall, angry at herself for getting them into this mess. She held Jack's pocketknife in her hand, her thumb rubbing the engraved words across the flat surface.

To my partner. Mike.

She had a feeling this Mike meant a lot to Jack. "Here's your knife," she told him, folding the silver blade into its case and tossing it to him.

"Thanks." Jack slid it in his jeans pocket.

"Who's Mike?" she asked, surprising herself that she even cared.

If the question bothered him, he didn't let on. "My partner."

"When you were on the police force?"

Although his face wasn't readable, his eyes were. Mike meant a lot to him. "Yeah."

"I take it you're friends, too."

Those dark eyes bored into her. "Now, who's the one probing?"

"Just making conversation," she said.

He glared at her. "Okay, Mike was my partner on the force…and yeah, we were friends."

"Were?"

He tensed and glanced away. "He was killed five years ago."

"Oh, Jack, I'm sorry."

He waved it off. "Forget it."

For a long time Willow didn't say anything. How could she forget it? She knew what it was like to lose someone you cared about. Her father's death had been devastating, but at least they'd been prepared during his long illness. She'd been able to spend time with him, they reminisced about things. She learned how much he loved the business, especially this last miniseries.

"Is Mike the reason you quit the police force?" She surprised herself by asking.

For a long time Jack didn't answer. "He was a big part of it. It wasn't the same after…" He stood and climbed on the bunk and began to examine the barred window.

"I already checked," Willow said as she stood beside him. "The bolts are the same." She felt his arms brush hers. She tried to move out of the way, but the unsteady mattress kept her close.

"Damn. This is even worse than the door." He rattled the solid bars. "Your father carried realism too far."

"There's nothing wrong with that." She faced him. Suddenly she realized how near he was. "He prided himself on that," she managed. "He loved the history of the old west."

"That sure as hell isn't going to help us now." He climbed down from the bunk and began to pace the small area.

"Someone is bound to come and look for us," she told him, trying to remain calm herself.

"How can they when no one knows we came here?"

"Maybe not, but getting all worked up isn't helping." She plopped down on the bunk.

Jack could see through Willow's brave act. She didn't like this situation any more than he did. He paced to control his anger. It burned him that the trusty foreman, Adams, would probably be the one to find them.

Calmer, he sat down on the floor, and leaned against the bars. "Mike would laugh at this."

She looked up. "Was he your partner for long?"

"Only about two years, but I knew him a long time before that." He smiled more to himself. "Let's just say I had several run-ins with him during my teen years. Mike was the cop in my neighborhood where I grew up."

"So he kind of looked out for you."

"Or busted my chops when I screwed up."

That got a smile from her. "And I bet you gave him a bad time."

"On my good days." Jack had had a lot of good days with Mike. "He got me into programs to keep me off the streets."

Taking off her hat, she stretched out on the mattress and propped her head in her hand. "I bet you were a force to be reckoned with?"

He was surprised at her assessment. "Maybe, but so was Mike. He let it be known that Underhill Street was his turf. We had to play by his rules."

"So did you?"

He stole a glance at her wide eyes and nearly lost it. She was getting to him. "Yeah. I did." He had to do something. "What about you? I bet you and your father were close."

She glanced away. "We were. After college, I went to work on his miniseries. He wasn't always an easy man when it came to the business." She played with the ragged edge of the blanket. "He was a perfectionist."

"I bet you did just fine."

"Not always. Whether I wanted to or not, it was hard to live in the limelight." Her eyes filled. "Every move any of us made seemed to end up in the newspaper. And people used you…. When you think you love some-one…someone you can trust…then realize it's because they want something."

Jack had read all about her opportunistic fiancé. Had that been what she meant when she said she hadn't been the perfect daughter. He scooted closer to the bunk, wondering how someone could hurt her like that.

"I'm sorry he hurt you, Willow." He meant it.

She shrugged. "It was a long time ago."

He reached out a finger and touched her lips. "He's not worth it, Willow. You're lucky to be rid of him." No name needed to be mentioned, they both knew who he was talking about.

"It caused trouble between me and my dad."

"That's because you're his daughter and he wanted to protect you."

A tear fell on the blanket. "I know, but I let him down."

Another tear escaped and he lost it. He got up, and lifted her into his arms as he sat on the bunk. "Oh, Willow. I doubt you could let anyone down." He cradled her close. He had no business doing this, but he couldn't seem to stop himself.

Jack couldn't breathe as he felt every inch of her trim body against his. He wanted nothing more than to keep her there. Then she raised her head, her hair wild and her eyes wide.

Jack groaned as his body took notice of her soft curves. "This is going to get us into a lot of trouble."

Her gaze locked with his, and he could see desire mirrored in those azure depths. Suddenly there wasn't enough blood flowing to his brain for him to form a coherent sentence. Only crazy thoughts. Like how her slender body fit his perfectly. How easy it would be to lean down and take her mouth.

He'd never before wanted to kiss a woman so badly.

"Damn, you tempt a man." He paused for a few beats of his pounding heart, then cupped the back of her head and pulled her closer. "Too much."

Jack brushed his lips across hers. She gasped, but didn't pull away. He took it as an invitation and raised up to meet her mouth again. This time he quickly deepened the kiss, running his tongue along the seam of her lips. She opened on a sigh, letting him slip inside to taste her. She returned his fervor and stroked her tongue against his. They were both being swept away by the moment.

He moved his hand across her back to bring her closer when suddenly someone called her name.

"Willow! Willow!"

At the sound of Trevor's voice, Jack pulled back and groaned. "Looks like you've been rescued…."

Willow kept her eyes diverted as she climbed to her feet and grabbed her hat. Her body was still humming from contact with Jack's. What was wrong with her? Just because he had sexy, bedroom eyes and a six-foot-two muscular build didn't mean she should have let him kiss her, or let her physical response to him nearly overwhelm her common sense.

She had to keep her focus on the family, the ranch… not a man who could destroy it all.

Still shaky from the kiss, she looked in Jack's direction. But before anything could be said, she heard Trevor call to her again.

She climbed on the bunk and called out the window, "Trevor, we're in the jail."

Seconds later they heard the foreman's booted feet on the wooden sideway, then the office door opened.

"Willow." He went to the cell door. "What are you doing in here?"

She pointed to the floor. "Just get the key, Trevor."

Trevor grabbed the key and unlocked the door. Willow stepped out; behind her came Jack.

"How did you get locked in?"

"We went inside and I backed into the door." Her voice was a little shaky. And why not? Hadn't she just let a stranger kiss the daylights out of her? "Give me the key." She took it and locked the cell door. "It isn't going to happen again."

"You shouldn't have been up here in the first place."

"Why? I wanted to show Jack around Liberty."

"You could have let someone know. When I got back with the horses and discovered you weren't back, I got worried."

"I'm sorry. And thank you for coming to look for us." She stole a glance at Jack. He didn't look the least bit uncomfortable.

Jack wasn't crazy about the foreman's attitude, worried or not. "Yeah, there are some pretty interesting places around here," he said.

Trevor ignored Jack and returned to Willow. "There are things that need your attention back at the ranch. And Bonnie Harris called from Fairhaven House." Trevor glanced at Jack again. The foreman didn't trust him. Jack couldn't blame him. If the situations were reversed he would be acting the same way.

"I'll call her," Willow promised.

Trevor adjusted his hat. "Are you heading back?" he asked.

"Planned on it," she said. "You go on, we'll be close behind."

Trevor nodded, then pointed a finger at Jack. "And you have to finish in the tack room."

"It'll get done," Jack said.

Without another word Adams climbed on his horse and rode off.

"That guy isn't happy with me here," Jack said.

"None of us are. We all want to be left alone."

"That's not the impression I got a few minutes ago."

"Believe me, there won't be a repeat of that." She started to walk away but he put a hand on her arm.

"I'm sorry, Willow. I took advantage of the situation. Let's chalk up the kiss as—"

"As a mistake," she finished for him.

He studied her, still feeling the aftershocks from their moment of closeness. "Okay. I'll go along with that. I think we both said and did things we wouldn't normally." His gaze went to her mouth. Her lips were slightly swollen, her cheeks flushed. She looked as if she'd been thoroughly kissed. He had to look away. "I want to thank you for today. I enjoyed the ride."

She offered a soft smile. "I hadn't been up here since Dad died. It brought back a lot of memories."

"Good ones, I hope."

"Yes, but today was almost a disaster. Never again." She slipped the cell key into her jeans pocket. "It's safer to keep the key put away, especially if any of the kids find their way here."

They walked back to the horses. Willow reached inside her saddlebag and pulled out her cell phone. "I probably should check to see what Bonnie wants. She screens the kids who get to come for camp." Willow punched in a code number and began to listen to her messages. "This should only take a few minutes."

"Go ahead," he told her as she walked away.

Jack watched Willow's expression suddenly change, then she turned away. His cop's instinct told him she was trying to hide something. Whose message besides Bonnie's was she listening to? Dean's maybe?

His temper flaring, he marched toward her. "Who called you?"

She blinked. "Excuse me?"

"Cut the innocent act, Willow. That was your brother, wasn't it?"

CHAPTER FOUR

WILLOW MANAGED to hold her temper as they rode back to the house. Just barely.

"You made a deal to tell me if Dean called you," Jack said.

"I'm not reneging on it, either. I didn't get a voice mail from Dean."

"Then let me listen to your voice mail."

"No. I'm not letting you go through my messages just because you don't believe me."

When they reached the corral gate, Willow swung her leg over Dakota's back and jumped to the ground. She marched to the gate and opened it before Jack got there.

"What have you got to hide?" he asked. He kept up with her fast pace.

"Nothing. But even you aren't going to invade my privacy."

She tugged on her horse's reins and walked into the barn, calling out for one of the ranch hands. Larry came out of a stall and she asked him to unsaddle Dakota and brush him down. Usually she loved to care for the stallion herself, but that joy had suddenly come to an end.

"I'm trying to help you," he said, pulling his horse along.

"You can help by caring for Cisco," she countered.

Willow turned and marched up to the house, desperately wanting to forget the man who'd kissed her senseless, and remember why he was really here. Her mother was with Gina in the kitchen planning supper. Not wanting to talk to anyone right now, Willow called out a greeting, but kept walking toward the stairs. She had to know if Dean was trying to send a message to her.

In the privacy of her bedroom, she took her phone from her pocket. Taking a deep breath and releasing it, she began to listen. Bonnie Harris came on the line.

"Willow. It's Bonnie.

"I need to talk with you about one of the children scheduled for camp. Is it possible for us to meet tomorrow…say later in the afternoon? I also want to finalize the list. There have been some changes."

Willow wrote down the number on a pad at her desk.

The next message was from a vendor who was supplying food for the camp. She took more notes then deleted the message.

There was one more message. After a long pause, a woman's voice said,

"Willow,

"You don't know me. My name is Heather. I need to talk to you about a…friend."

This was the call that she suspected had something to do with her brother. She had no idea who Heather was, but she knew that the number's area code came from Seattle. She jotted it down as a knock sounded on the door. Her mother popped in.

"Jack is downstairs," she said. "He wants to see you."

"Too bad. He can just wait."

"I don't think Jack Sullivan is the patient type." A hint of a smile appeared. "Did something happen?"

"Yes. He practically demanded to go through my personal messages."

Molly stood there a minute, then crossed the room to her daughter. "Has Dean called you, Willow?"

Willow shook her head. "No, but someone named Heather did. The call came from Seattle."

"Then maybe you should let Jack know about it."

"I would have, if he hadn't acted like…like some Neanderthal."

Her mother's eyes twinkled. "Jack can be intense, but he has a job to do. And we said we'd cooperate. So I think you should go and let him know what you learned."

"If he hadn't been so bossy, maybe I would have." She couldn't help remember how he took charge of the kiss. How his mouth moved over hers, stroking…

"Willow?"

Her mother took her by the hand and tugged her toward the door. "I'm sure Jack will apologize to you."

Together they went downstairs and found him pacing in the room. He stopped and met her at the base of the steps. "Okay, maybe I came off a little strong."

Willow arched an eyebrow. "A little?"

"And I apologize. Now, may I listen to your messages?"

His ebony gaze was mesmerizing, causing her anger to melt away. "I didn't hear from my brother."

He sighed. "But you got a suspicious message."

She nodded. "There's a call from someone named Heather who wants to talk to me. Her phone number has a Seattle area code."

He held out his hand. "May I listen to it?"

She hesitated, trying to recall the man she'd been locked in the cell with. The lost look in his eyes when she'd asked about Mike. He was the same man whose touch made her feel desire…and his kiss made her feel hunger.

She pushed away the memory. All she wanted to believe was that Jack was being truthful when he told her Dean was in trouble. And right now, he might be her brother's only chance. Willow punched in her password, then handed him the cell phone.

Jack listened, then grabbed the pen off the oversize oak desk that had been her father's and jotted down the number. He handed the phone back to her. "Did you call Heather?"

"No," Willow admitted. "But I think she knows Dean."

He nodded. "Stan Walsh's daughter's name is Heather."

Willow was more angry than surprised. "You knew Dean was involved with his boss's daughter?"

"Yes."

"You didn't think we should know this? Did you think that maybe Heather's father might not want his daughter involved with one of his employees? Is that the reason he's after Dean?"

He shook his head. "No, that's not the reason."

Willow rubbed her temples. "Okay, I'm grasping here, but I still don't believe that my brother is guilty of anything bad enough for a P.I. to come looking for him." She stared at him. "Is he?"

"Let's take it one step at a time. First, Willow, you need to call Heather."

"Wait! You need to tell us what kind of trouble Dean's in."

He hesitated. "Okay. There's company money missing. And all signs point to Dean."

Willow began to shake. "Dean wouldn't steal," she told him. "Mother, tell him Dean wouldn't steal."

Molly kept her composure. "Jack, until you show me proof, I believe in my son's innocence."

"That's the reason we need more information to find out for sure. So you need to call Heather." He went to the desk phone. "Use the landline and I'll tape it with the recorder."

Willow finally sat down in the leather chair. "What do I say to her?"

"Just let her do the talking," he instructed. "She called you, and if she knows where Dean is maybe she can get a message to him."

Willow was nervous as she looked at her mother. She wanted to know where her brother was, but she also wanted him safe. She punched in the numbers then listened as the phone rang.

"Hello," a woman's voice said.

"Is this Heather?"

"Yes it is. Willow?"

"Yes." Willow took a breath. "Heather, do you know my brother, Dean Kingsley?"

"Yes…" There was a long pause until finally Heather spoke. "Willow, I'm afraid for him," the girl said, tears in her voice. "My dad is so angry, he won't listen to me."

"Heather, I know Dean's in trouble, but you have to tell me what happened."

"Dean didn't do anything wrong. Someone made it look like it was him. Someone else took the money."

Willow felt a certain amount of relief. "Who took the money?" She glanced at Jack. "And why was Dean blamed?"

"It's all my fault." Heather began to cry. "And now Dean's in trouble because of me."

"Tell me why you think that."

"I can't talk anymore."

"Heather, tell Dean to call me." The line went dead. "She hung up."

Jack hit the stop button and played the conversation back so they all could listen.

"Poor dear, she sounded heartbroken," Willow's mother said.

"What if what she said is true?" Willow asked as she glanced at Jack. "That someone set up Dean?"

Jack was questioning it, too, more than he should. Hell, he was hired to find Kingsley and nothing more. Not to try to figure out his guilt or innocence. He needed to get his perspective back, not think about the suspect's sexy sister.

"Then he has to go and prove his innocence."

"Even if Walsh just wants a pound of flesh because of his daughter?" Willow asked.

Jack knew she wanted someone to blame. "As I said, I know for a fact the money is gone. And everything points to Dean."

Willow exchanged a worried glance with her mother. "That's convenient."

* * *

Jack held his words until Molly excused herself and left the room, then he turned to Willow. "I don't like you insinuating that I helped set up Dean." He took a breath. No one questioned his integrity. "I don't work that way. For one, it's illegal, and for another, I could lose my license and go to jail."

"I didn't mean you," she said. "Someone else at the company could have taken the money and put the blame on Dean."

He relaxed some, but it bothered him that she thought so little of him. "I should get back to work. Let me know if anything else turns up," he called over his shoulder as he turned to leave.

He hadn't even reached the door when he felt her hand grip his arm. "Jack, please. I said I was sorry. You just made me so angry to think I'd hide my brother's call from you."

She was standing so close, Jack couldn't avoid her eyes. That was his first mistake. If possible, the blue turned a richer hue. The second was to let her nearness affect him. Then suddenly he wanted to repeat what happened earlier, and kiss her inviting mouth. "Look, I'm caught between a rock and a hard place here. I was hired to find Dean."

"Even if my brother isn't guilty?" she insisted.

He tried to ignore her. Her featherlight touch shot all the way through his body, slammed into his heart…and his stomach…and lower.

"You don't know that for sure. It's best for everyone if your brother comes forward."

"So the media can crucify him?" She sighed. "Dean got into some trouble in his youth. Believe me, Jack, people don't forget." Her gaze held his. "And what about my mother? She's just been able to start looking forward to things…."

Jack didn't want to feel anything for her, but he did. It had been a long time since a woman distracted him. He had to fight it. "Innocent people get hurt all the time, Willow. I know all too well. Sometimes it can't be helped. Don't sell your mother short, she's tougher than she looks."

"You've never had to deal with the media."

Wrong. He thought back to the robbery that had gone bad. The day Mike got shot. Then again at the trial when the shooter walked away free. He tensed. It would always eat at him that a guilty man went free that day. And he refused to let it happen again.

"Just because your family has notoriety and money doesn't mean your brother gets special attention."

Her back straightened. "I'm not asking for any special treatment. Just that you listen to Dean's side before you judge him. Unless it's all about getting the job done and collecting the money." She tossed that wild mane of hair and started to walk by him.

She finally pushed him too far. He reached out and grabbed her.

"You have no idea what you're talking about. You get special attention just because of being Matt Kingsley's daughter. As a cop, I've seen it happen too many times." The emotions churned his insides out. "The worst was a twenty-year veteran cop who lost his life because his killer came from a wealthy family."

She gasped. "Mike?"

He nodded. "Yeah, my partner died in my arms the

day a punk teenager pointed a gun and thought nothing about taking a life."

Her eyes widened in pain. "Oh, Jack, I'm sorry."

"Yeah, so am I. I guess that makes me a little cynical."

She didn't back down as she glared at him. "Yes, you are, but you can't judge my brother like that, you don't even know him."

"Then get Dean to talk to me. I'll listen to his side."

Her eyes widened. "Really?"

He nodded. "But understand, I'm still obligated to tell Walsh if I find Dean."

"I was hoping for more time." She forced a smile. "But I'll take it." She escaped his hold and walked out, leaving Jack to feel as if he should be doing more.

The next evening, Willow said goodbye to Bonnie in the parking lot of an out-of-the-way restaurant in Pasadena. They'd worked the past two hours, only stopping for a chef's salad as they finalized arrangements for the summer camp. The list of kids who qualified had to have their medical releases, and the parent consent forms completed for the Wandering Creek liability insurance. It was all done.

Now, the only thing left was to contact the publicity agent to work on a press release for opening day, hoping it would help raise money for both Fairhaven House and Kingsley's Kids charities.

Her mother had already hosted several fund-raisers, but they had to keep the public focused on the kids' needs. And it was never too soon to plan for next year.

The June evening had cooled down and Willow pulled

her sweater closer as she walked to her car. That was when she noticed a man leaning against a vehicle, watching her. She automatically tensed, remembering all the years photographers had followed the family around. After her father's death, it slowed down, but Scott had loved the attention. He craved it. After she'd discovered her fiancé's agenda, she broke off their engagement. Her heart still ached when she recalled how he'd gotten back at her.

Even eighteen months later, the tabloid pictures and stories still hurt. She hoped by now Willow Kingsley would be old news. She had no social life…no drug problem…no man in her life.

Willow hurried to her vintage red '66 Ford Mustang. A present from her father at college graduation. He'd been a big car buff, and she'd shared that love with him.

With a smile, she unlocked the door and climbed inside. She checked her mirror to see that the man had gotten into his vehicle, too. She let it go as coincidence, and decided to bypass the freeway and traffic for a more scenic route home. She enjoyed the winding road that skirted the San Gabriel Mountains.

It wasn't as if she had anywhere else to be tonight. Her mother wasn't even home waiting. She'd gone to spend a few days in Santa Barbara with friends. Willow thought about her own social life. Not that she'd ever been a socialite, but lately, it was nonexistent.

Her thoughts turned to Jack. He was so different from any man she'd known before. He had far too many rough edges…and was far too dangerous for her taste. Yet, she was intrigued.

She recalled what he'd told her about his father not

being in his childhood. The trouble he'd gotten into with the law. Yet Jack had grown up and become a police officer. Willow thought about her own parents. Their love had been a mainstay in her youth. Who had been there for Jack? She knew the answer to that—Mike.

She gripped the wheel of her car, remembering their time together yesterday. Whether she liked it or not, she'd been drawn to him. A shiver ran through her at the memory of his touch…the intense look in those sexy bedroom eyes. The way his mouth…

She shook her head. "Stop it. He's going after Dean." She glanced in her rearview mirror to see the same car from the parking lot had followed her off the main highway.

The media wanted something newsworthy. Now with Kingsley's Kids back in the news was she going to be tailed everywhere she went?

She wasn't in the mood to talk to the media. She checked the road ahead, catching the golden hue over the mountains. Nothing like a California sunset… except maybe someone to share it with.

It was dusk and she flipped on her lights; her attention went back to guiding her little sports car along the curves. Uneasiness crept through her as she stole another glance in the mirror again. The other car had kept up. She downshifted at the next curve, then quickly pressed on the accelerator coming out, hoping to gain some momentum and distance. She didn't see the oncoming car as she drifted into its path and the headlights blinded her.

She screamed at the same time she jerked the wheel to avoid hitting the vehicle and headed for the embankment.

Jack dropped his head back on his pillow. He'd been on the phone with Stan Walsh, but in their thirty-minute conversation, Jack had neglected to mention Walsh's daughter had called Willow. He'd kept that information to himself, hoping Heather would call back and disclose Dean's location.

Or was it because of Willow?

Jack shut his eyes, thinking about the woman with the big blue eyes and pretty smile. Definitely, he'd let the suspect's sister cloud his mind and his judgment. Never before had he gotten personally involved with anyone during a job. Or allowed anyone to make him lose his professional focus on a case. And kissing her was way out of line.

He got up and walked to the window. He could hear the other men in the main room playing poker. He had been, too, but he couldn't concentrate on the cards. After losing twenty bucks he decided to call it a night.

Jack looked at the night sky, thinking about Mike. "I know you're laughing now, old buddy. You said I'd find her one day." He sighed. "Doesn't matter how I feel. She's so out of my league."

His cell phone rang, bringing him out of his reverie. He grabbed it off the nightstand and flipped it open. "Sullivan."

"Jack…" a soft voice whispered.

"Willow?" Why was she calling him? "Is something wrong?"

"I couldn't get ahold of Trevor." She paused. "I sort of had an accident."

Oh, God! "Are you hurt?"

"Not too bad. I guess…I was more scared. Jack…"

She said his name and his chest tightened. "Willow, tell me where are you. I'll come get you."

"I'm at a small hospital." She gave him directions.

He was already walking out of his room and through the door to the bunkhouse. "I'm on my way."

"Just to warn you, there are newspeople outside."

"I'm a big boy, I can handle them. I'll protect you, Willow." He jumped into his truck, realizing his hand was a little shaky. He had to pull himself together before he faced Willow.

Thirty minutes later, Jack arrived at the emergency room. He walked inside to find several people milling around. How many were from the media? He didn't care. He went straight to the middle-aged woman at the desk.

She glanced at him. "May I help you?"

Jack leaned forward and said quietly, "I'm Jack Sullivan for Willow Kingsley."

She nodded, then motioned for him to follow her. She led him down a corridor then into a room. "Ms. Kingsley is behind the last curtain."

"Thank you."

She finally smiled. "I was a big fan of Matt Kingsley." She turned and left.

Jack wasn't sure what he'd find as he walked around the curtain. He relaxed, seeing Willow on the bed dressed in a hospital gown. She had a bandage on her forehead and a scrape across her cheek and her leg elevated with an ice bag on her ankle.

"Willow?"

She looked at him; her smile was wobbly. "You came."

He went to her, fighting to keep from pulling her into his arms. "Looks like you got in a fight." His gaze zoned in on hers. "What happened?"

She shrugged. "I swerved to miss a car and ran off the road. Then everything went kind of blurry."

His heart pounded hard. "You were unconscious?"

"Not totally. I remember a man came to my door and helped me out. Climbing back to the road, I twisted my ankle." She nodded toward her leg. "He called an ambulance and the police came…." With a sigh, her eyes met his. "I think it was my fault. I wrecked my Mustang."

His gaze roamed over her beautiful face. "All that matters is you're safe."

She bit down on her lower lip and nodded. "I know it's crazy, but my dad gave me that car." Tears filled her eyes.

"I believe your father would care more about your safety, than a vehicle."

"Someone was following me, Jack, and I'm pretty sure it was a photographer. I was trying to lose him."

"Dammit, Willow. You could have really been hurt." The hell with it. He sat down on the bed, and drew her into his arms.

"Jack, what if they found out about Dean?" Her words were muffled against his chest.

"You can't worry about that now, Willow." A shudder ran through him when he pulled back and assessed her scrapes and bruises. "Let's get you out of here. Where's the doctor?"

Willow watched as Jack went off. She almost called him back, wanting that secure feeling he'd caused in her the second he'd walked in. It had been a long time since she'd relied on anyone, and she was probably crazy to trust this man…but she did.

She heard Jack's voice again as he returned with the young doctor. "Well, Ms. Kingsley—" he began going over her chart "—your X-rays show no broken bones, but you do have a sprained ankle. You need to stay off of it for a day or so." He hesitated. "I am a little concerned about your concussion, but Mr. Sullivan assured me he can handle your care."

Willow blinked and looked at Jack. "I have a housekeeper at home, too."

The doctor nodded. "I'll write you a prescription for pain."

"Fine." She scooted to the side of the bed. "I just want to go home."

The doctor left as a nurse came in with her belongings.

Jack looked at her. "I'll wait for you out in the hall." He walked out.

Immediately, the nurse gave her a pill for the pain, then helped her into her clothes. She didn't look much better dressed in her bloodstained T-shirt and sweater. She brushed her hair carefully and added some lip gloss.

Jack returned. "I moved my car to the back door."

"Thank you," she said as he slipped his arm around her and helped her into a wheelchair and pushed her down the corridor. His SUV was just outside the glass door. But so were a group of photographers.

"Damn," Jack murmured. "Hang on. I'll get you through this." He opened the door and moved her outside.

"Willow," they called in unison. "Tell us what happened to you. Did someone run you off the road? Were you drinking?"

Willow put her hand up to shield her face.

Jack opened the passenger side door and guided Willow into the car. "Ms. Kingsley has no comment," he said. "Now, if you'll excuse us, she would like to go home."

"Willow…who's the new man in your life?" a female reporter called out. Jack didn't stop, just gently lifted her into the passenger seat. Willow kept her face turned away from the cameras.

Jack moved through the crowd and climbed in the driver's side. Silently, he started the engine and managed to drive out of the parking lot.

The effects of the pill were helping with Willow's headache, but the medication was also making things a little fuzzy. "Thank you for coming to get me."

"Not a big deal," Jack told her.

"It is a big deal. If Mom had to come and get me the media…"

He smiled. "I've said it before, she would've handled it."

That made Willow smile, too. "What about you? Can you handle being the new man in my life?"

He glanced toward her. "Yeah, I can handle it."

CHAPTER FIVE

JACK PUNCHED IN the numbers at the security gate at the ranch. He glanced across the car, glad to see Willow was asleep, and not in pain. Now, all he had to do was get her into the house…and into bed.

He pulled the car into the driveway at the back door. He glanced toward the bunkhouse. There weren't any lights on. Good, he didn't need to deal with Trevor as he tried to get Willow inside and up to her room. He walked around to the passenger side and opened the door. He slipped his arms under her legs and across her back, then lifted her into his arms.

She opened her eyes momentarily. "Jack…"

"It's okay, sweetheart. Go back to sleep. I'll have you in bed soon."

She blinked. "You're taking me to bed?"

"That's right."

She smiled. "Good."

His body tightened, but he ignored the feeling and went to the porch. He looked inside to see Gina in the kitchen and tapped on the glass.

She hurried to open the French doors. "Oh, my. Mr. Sullivan, what happened to Willow?"

"She's okay, Gina. She had a car accident and the doctor gave her pain medication. I need to get her into bed." Jack walked through the house and started up the stairs.

Gina rushed after him. "Her room is the last door." Gina led the rest of the way and stopped at the end of the hall, then opened the door, and flicked on the light. Jack followed her inside and waited until the housekeeper pulled back a satiny blue comforter. He laid Willow down on the white sheets.

"Should I call Mrs. Kingsley?"

Jack shook his head. "I don't want her driving home in the middle of the night. Besides, Willow doesn't want to worry her." He went and pulled off Willow's sandals, then looked at her jeans and T-shirt. "Maybe you could get her undressed and into something more comfortable."

The pretty dark-haired girl nodded, and Jack left the room. Ten minutes later, he returned to find Willow half-awake.

"Jack… You're still here," she said softly.

He sat down on the side of the bed. "Someone has to look out for you." He took out a pin light. "I need to check your pupils." She let him shine the light in her eyes.

She blinked and said sleepily, "Well, how am I?"

"You're fine." He glanced at Gina standing in the doorway and nodded.

"Willow," the housekeeper said and came into the room. "You want me to get you anything…call any-one? Trevor?"

"Oh, no, Gina," Willow said. "Don't call Trevor. He worked all day supervising the cabin repairs."

Gina looked at Jack. He knew she was sending him a warning. She finally walked out, leaving the door ajar.

He turned his attention back to the patient. "I'm going to have to wake you up in a few hours."

She groaned. "I feel so sleepy."

"Then rest now."

Her lashes fluttered. "Will you be here?"

He nodded, not trusting himself to speak.

"Good." She ran her tongue around her lips. "These pills make me feel funny."

"That means they're doing their job." He suddenly thought about how she was banged around in the car.

The room was in dim light, but he could see her gaze.

"Am I your job, Jack? Is that why you're here?"

Jack knew Willow didn't trust easily. "I'm here because you need me." He brushed a strand of hair off her forehead. "It has nothing to do with my job."

She smiled and his gut tightened. "I'm glad." She poked a finger at his chest. "I like you Jack 'Sully' Sullivan. You're not such a bad guy."

He frowned. "Don't be too sure of that."

"Oh, you talk tough," she murmured as her hand wandered over his chest. He felt her heat. "But I know…I know better."

It would be wise if he got up and left, but he couldn't. He liked her hand on him. He wanted to stay close to her. "What do you know?"

"I know that you watched me."

Ouch, he'd been caught. "You're pretty easy on the

eyes." He leaned closer, close enough that he could kiss her. And he already knew how dangerous that could be. Of course he'd always been attracted to risky things. But how low could a man get, taking advantage of her weakened condition?

She smiled. "So are you. You know what else? I've been thinking a lot about the kiss." She drifted off a moment, then she opened her eyes. "You do remember it, don't you?"

"Far too often," he confessed.

"So do I. I liked it, too. I liked when you kissed me, Jack." She closed her eyes again, this time for good.

Jack watched her sleep for a moment, then got up and went to the window. He convinced himself that by morning Willow wouldn't remember a thing about tonight.

Too bad he wouldn't forget.

Willow blinked her eyes as the sunlight poured across her bed. With a groan, she rolled over to escape the bright glare. She also wanted to escape the dull pain in her head, and the aches in her body. Suddenly memories from last night rushed back. The drive home, the blinding headlights coming toward her…then the police, the hospital. Jack.

She opened her eyes, sat up and looked around the room. The familiar space was orderly and there was no evidence that Jack Sullivan had been here.

Was he a dream? She shivered, recalling the man who'd been so gentle with her…who took care of her through the night. No, she definitely was in an accident. Her entire body ached. And she definitely remembered Jack's touch. Willow closed her eyes also remembering how chatty she'd been in her drug-induced state.

There was a soft knock on the door and her mother peered inside. "Good morning, Willow."

"Mom, you're home." She frowned. "Did Gina call you?"

"If you must know, it was Jack." Sitting down on the bed, she reached out and stroked her daughter's cheek. "I should have been here with you." Tears clouded her mother's eyes. "You could have been hurt badly."

Willow hated that she'd worried her. "I'm sorry, Mom. I was more concerned about you having to deal with the media. They must have heard about the accident on the police scanner. They were at the hospital."

Molly smiled and tiny lines appeared around her eyes. "Jack told me. I'm glad he managed to get you home safely. I'm grateful he was here for you."

Willow was, too. She couldn't forget how he held her, not leaving her side. Then reality returned. "He's still after Dean."

"We're all looking for Dean." Her mother straightened. "I'm not happy about his decision to hide out." This time the tears were there. "I love my son, but he's an adult and running away isn't going to solve any problem."

"I want to help him, too."

Molly gripped her hand. "We all do, Willow. Your dad and I had countless arguments about Dean's wrong choices. As a parent it's always hard to know what's the right thing to do for your child." Her mother sighed. "As much as I'd love to try and handle this problem, I can't.

Dean is the one who has to prove he's innocent. And in the end, he'll be a better man for it."

Willow nodded. "If Jack would stop…"

Her mother arched an eyebrow. "Doing his job? Disturbing your life?"

More than you know. "He has more or less moved in."

"At our invitation. And he's been working pretty hard, too. Not to mention that he came to your rescue last night."

Willow couldn't deny that. He'd been the first person she called. "But he still works for Mr. Walsh."

"And just maybe Jack will dig a little deeper into finding other employees who might have set up Dean." Molly's gaze held hers. "Maybe you should ask him to help."

Willow didn't want to owe Jack Sullivan any more than she already did. "I think I need to concentrate on the five dozen campers arriving at the end of the week."

"You need to concentrate on healing."

"I'm fine. My ankle is just a little tender. I need to get up and shower. Those pain pills make everything fuzzy."

Molly smiled. "Jack said you were a little out of it. And that you were upset you wrecked the Mustang."

"Oh, I need to call the insurance company and see if the car can be fixed."

Her mother stood. "No, you need to take it easy for a while. Just a shower, nothing more." She pointed to the desk and a pair of crutches. "Maybe you should use those. Do you want help?"

Willow stood up slowly. Her ankle was a little tender, but she could walk on it. "I'm fine."

Her mother went to the door. "When you've finished, come down for breakfast. Jack will be joining us."

Great. Willow tried not to react as she went to her dresser and took out clean underwear. The man had managed to get into her life…for now. But she drew the line at letting him into her heart.

Willow made her way down the stairs, being careful of her ankle. At the base of the steps, she heard laughter ring out. The sound came from the kitchen. She stopped short in the doorway to see the foursome at the table.

Jack, Molly, Trevor and Gina were talking and seemed to be enjoying themselves. Finally Trevor looked up and saw her.

"Willow." He hurried to her, eyeing the bandage on her forehead. "Hey, how are you doing?"

"Fine. Just a little sore."

"You should have called me," her longtime friend said.

"I think your cell phone was off," she told him. "Besides you'd worked all day on the cabins."

He studied her. "So you called Sullivan?"

"Don't go giving me grief, Trevor…"

"I'm not. Gina told me how he brought you home and stayed with you to make sure you were okay." He glanced over his shoulder. "So…maybe he's not such a bad guy. And he told Molly he'd be looking deeper into Dean's case as soon as he got back to Seattle."

Jack was leaving?

Trevor led her to the table and pulled out a chair across from Jack. He'd cleaned up, too, and changed into a tan shirt and jeans.

"How are you feeling this morning?" he asked.

"Pretty good." Her gaze met his. How many times

had he looked into her eyes last night? She shivered, re-calling his husky voice, his arousing touch.

"No headache this morning?"

She sank into her chair, feeling everyone's attention on her. "Just a little." Gina placed a glass of juice in front of her. She took a long drink. "What's going on?"

Jack shrugged. "We were discussing camp activities."

"Yeah, Willow." Trevor came to the table. "Jack was telling us stories about his summer camp days. He's come up with an idea."

She turned to Jack. Those dark eyes locked on her. She felt herself tremble. "Ideas about what?"

Jack shrugged. "I was just thinking out loud."

"How about letting me hear some of your thoughts?" she asked. She didn't want to be left out.

"Okay. I suggested that since you have Liberty, why not do a Western Days reenactment with the kids?"

Molly joined in. "And I thought why not go further and film it…make a movie. I still have some friends in the business who will probably be able to volunteer some of their time. Your father's production company still has a lot of the equipment and costumes from his series. Who knows, we might find we have a budding Clint Eastwood, or Steven Spielberg?"

Willow saw the excitement in her mother's eyes. "That's a huge undertaking, Mom. Do you think there's time before camp opens?"

She waved her hand. "I'm not afraid of hard work. Besides, this could give these kids some hope…a future. If this works this year, we could expand the program." She grinned. "Oh, and it could be so much fun. I know there's a dozen or so of your father's scripts around. With a little editing, one of them could work for these kids. If anything the campers will get a kick out of seeing themselves on film."

Molly set her fork down. "Gina, I'm going to need an assistant. And, Trevor, you, too."

The two exchanged a glance and Willow wondered if her family had gone crazy. The conversation continued during breakfast, then after Trevor and Gina followed Molly into the office. Leaving Willow alone with Jack.

Jack could see that Willow was uncomfortable about the previous night. He wished she wasn't, because he enjoyed every minute with her. This morning it had been difficult to leave her.

"So you do feel all right? No headache, really?"

"Yes." She concentrated on her food. "I took some ibuprofen when I got up. I'm a little sore."

He nodded. "You probably should stay off your ankle…so it won't swell again." She still didn't look at him. "Willow. I don't want you to feel awkward about last night."

She finally looked at him. "The drugs made me say things."

He smiled. "I know…"

Her face reddened. "I hope I didn't do anything…"

"You mean take advantage of me? I wish. But no, you were a perfect lady."

"I doubt that." She got up and went to the counter to refill her coffee mug. "I said a lot of crazy things, Jack."

Although he shouldn't be, Jack was drawn to Willow Kingsley. Big-time. He got up and went to her. "I didn't think anything you said was crazy, Willow. You were honest," he told her. "You said you liked our kiss. Well, I enjoyed it, too."

He took her by the shoulders and turned her around. She raised her head and those clear blue eyes were intoxicating.

"Jack… We can't."

"Can't what…? Have these feelings? Then tell me how to stop, Willow."

She closed her eyes. "You're going after Dean. My family has to come first."

He cursed softly. "You don't know how badly I want to forget everything else…." His hand touched her cheek.

"I wish that, too."

She closed her eyes and he couldn't resist. He kissed her, covering her surprised gasp with his mouth. That was about all the resistance she gave him as her arms slid up his chest and around his neck. She opened to him, and he delved into her warmth and sweetness. But he still couldn't get enough of her. And for the first time in his life he didn't just desire a woman, he wanted more…. He was afraid he might not be able to walk away this time.

Jack broke off the kiss. They both had trouble catching their breath. "There's something happening between us." He stroked her hair. "The last thing I want to do is hurt you."

She tried to pull away. "But with you looking for my brother…it's bound to happen."

Jack wouldn't let her go. "Maybe I'll be the one who gets hurt, Willow. I still have a job to do. If I don't find your brother, someone else will. The only difference is if it's me, that will always be between us."

"It isn't fair...."

"I learned a long time ago life isn't always fair."

Willow wanted to push the entire world away and stay in Jack's arms. She knew he was right...about everything. Her family had to be her concern.

He stared at her. "And I have to do my job."

"So that leaves us on opposite sides."

He nodded. "But that doesn't mean we can't help each other." He was crazy to even think about getting involved in this. "I told you, you help me find Dean, I'll listen to what he has to say and look into the possibility that someone set him up. I'll get access to other employees in his department." He pointed a finger at her. "It's a long shot, Willow, and you need to help, too. Call Heather. See if she has any leading suspects."

Willow was so excited. "You could lose your job."

"I'll still be looking for Dean, but isn't it better if we get the right person?"

"Is this because of Mike?"

Jack's expression changed to sadness. "It's because I want to see the guilty pay. I'll never try to railroad your brother."

She believed that. "Thank you."

He frowned. "Don't thank me yet. Dean's still in a lot of trouble."

Before Willow could say more the phone rang. She went to answer it. "Hello. Kingsley residence."

"Ms. Kingsley, this is Bill Higgins, your insurance agent. We just looked over the damage to your car."

"How bad is it?" she asked.

"It doesn't look good, but we're going to authorize the repairs."

"That's wonderful news. Thank you, Mr. Higgins. Goodbye." She hung up the phone still smiling. "They're going to be able to fix the Mustang."

Jack found himself grinning, too. "That's great news. If you need a good body shop, I know of one in L.A."

Why wasn't Willow surprised? "How is that possible?"

"A few years back, I did some security work for the owner. You might have heard of Classic Details."

She blinked. "Yeah, it's got quite a reputation as the best body shop in the L.A. area, that is if I don't want my car back anytime soon."

"When you want something done well, it should take time." He wasn't thinking about cars. "I mean you want the job to be thorough…." He should shut his mouth. He pulled out the business card with the garage's phone number on the back. "Just call and ask for Dave, then mention my name."

Willow went to the phone and punched in the numbers. When Dave answered the phone she told him the problem. He said he'd look at the car and let her know. When she said Jack's name, Dave's attitude changed. He promised to get back to her by the end of the day.

She hung up when the newspaper on the counter caught her eye. "He told me to have my Mustang towed over and he'd call me before five," she said as she examined the grainy photograph of Jack helping her into the car at the hospital. "Thank you," she said absently.

He tried to take the paper. "Not a problem."

She stopped him and retrieved the paper and glanced at the headlines. Willow Kingsley's Latest Cowboy. "Oh, no. Jack, I'm sorry." She tossed the paper in disgust. "I knew this would happen."

"Willow, it's okay." He smiled. "I can handle a little press. Beside the story isn't bad. It's not going to hurt the camp."

She nodded, embarrassed she'd put him in this position. "I better get back to work."

"Jack, you know that you don't need to work as a hand."

"What? And blow my cover?" He smiled. "I'm probably going to get some grief from not sleeping in my bunk." He couldn't help but move closer to her. "I don't want the men to think there's something going on between us."

"I've learned a long time ago, I can't control what people think," she said. "Thanks for getting me home last night."

His gaze settled on hers. He could get lost in those eyes. Whoever said blue was a cool color? Willow's blue eyes threw off pure heat.

"And for staying with me."

"Hell, Willow, that was the easy part. Leaving you early this morning was damn hard." He watched as she swallowed hard.

"I know I said some things…."

"You were pretty chatty." He leaned toward her. "But don't try to deny anything, because we both know you wanted me there as much as I wanted to be there." Her breath was soft against his cheek. He pressed his mouth against hers. She made a whimpering sound and he saw the desire in her eyes. Damn, she was so easy to read. He knew he could use it to his advantage, but right now he could only think about how much he wanted her. He dipped his head again and took another nip, then repeated it. His body ached like crazy, but he released her and walked away, before he lost it.

That'd never happened to him.

On Friday, Willow took one last ride on Dakota. The buses would arrive tomorrow morning, bringing sixty adolescent kids.

For the next two weeks, her life wouldn't be her own. She not only had to deal with the campers, but the media. And probably more questions about her accident…and Jack. Would they still want to know who he was? How could she answer that when she didn't know herself?

Willow needed Jack to remain the enemy, it was safer for her, but when he kissed her, she lost any resistance. But she couldn't. The man was here for only one reason, to get Dean. If he flirted with her, or kissed her again, she couldn't allow herself to think that it would lead to anything more. And she hoped the reporters would drop it, too.

Willow didn't want anything to detract from positive PR for the camp. It had been her father's dream, and now hers. Matt Kingsley's own bad childhood had made it easy for him to give underprivileged kids a chance. At least a nice summer away from their bad environment.

Now, the camp was up and running again. This time with a new program on the roster…the making of a movie. This had turned out to be her mother's pet project and she was blossoming with her job. Movie producer.

Since college Willow had worked alongside her father, helping to run the summer camp. It was going to be hard this year without his enthusiasm and guidance. And Dean's problem would be a big distraction.

Willow had done what Jack had asked and phoned Heather, numerous calls over the past few days, but no one had answered the cell phone. She'd left messages for Dean hoping she'd hear something. So far nothing.

Willow shifted in the saddle as she turned her attention back to her job. She checked out the half-dozen newly refurbished cabins, four that would be filled with kids and the other two with their counselors. She went to the next item on her checklist. There were plenty of fresh linens and towels stacked in the supply building. The general meeting hall where the campers ate meals was set up for tomorrow's orientation.

There were enough saddle horses to handle the most inexperienced riders. And hopefully enough food to feed five dozen hungry kids and six counselors.

She directed Dakota toward the covered bridge that arched over Golden Creek. When she reached the weathered wooden structure, she climbed down and tied the horse's reins to the post.

It was cool under the roof as slits of sunlight filtered through the overhead boards, illuminating her walk across the bridge. She came out on the other side and found a tree to sit beside. She gave herself a ten-minute reprieve before she had to get back to work.

That was when her cell phone went off. She pulled it out of her pocket, thinking it was Trevor wanting something.

She spoke into the phone. "What is it now?"

There was a long pause, then she recognized the voice. "Willow…"

"Dean?"

"Yeah, it's me, sis."

"Dean, where have you been?" Her voice trembled as she stood. "I've been calling you."

"I know. I know, sis. And I can't tell you where I am now because I don't want you to get in any trouble."

"Don't worry about me," she told him. "You're the one who's in trouble. Dean, you've got to go and talk to your boss."

"No. Walsh will just have me arrested. I didn't do anything, Willow. I'm innocent."

She allowed herself to smile. "I know, Dean. But you can't keep running. Look, Jack Sullivan is a private investigator who's working on the case—"

"And he works for Walsh," Dean interrupted.

"How did you know about Jack?"

There was a long pause. "Heather heard her father talking to him."

"Dean, I don't know what's going on, but Jack is going to try and look for other suspects. But you have to cooperate with him."

"What if it's a trap, Willow?"

Jack wouldn't do that, would he? "What if Jack can help you?" If she was wrong, her brother could go to prison. "But you've got to talk with him."

"I can't, Willow, not yet. I'm working on my own lead. I know who did this to me."

She circled the tree. "Dean, you can't do this on your own. Let us help."

"And when the media finds out, I can see the headlines. Matt Kingsley's Son In Trouble…Again. No, I don't think so. Look, Willow, I only need a few more days. Please. If I can't find anything, I'll let Sullivan take over."

Willow thought about the promise she'd made Jack, to let him know if Dean called her. Maybe Dean could find the lead that Jack needed, or maybe not. That wasn't his job. It was only two days. "You've got until Sunday."

There was a long pause. "I love you, sis." The phone went dead.

"What happens on Sunday?"

Willow swung around to find Jack walking toward her.

CHAPTER SIX

JACK HADN'T SEEN Willow since the morning after her accident. The last time he'd kissed her.

When he should have been concentrating on his job here, she'd been crowding his thoughts…distracting him. He was suspicious by nature and that made him wonder if she'd been completely honest with him.

He had trouble believing that Dean hadn't contacted his family, especially a sister who'd been his number one supporter. So when she'd taken off on Dakota at daybreak, he'd found an excuse to go after her.

"You're a hard woman to locate these days." He came down the bank to the edge of the shallow creek.

"Not that hard," she corrected. "I've been around."

Jack raised an eyebrow, eyeing her snug jeans, fitted blouse and cowboy hat. The same sexy cowgirl image had kept him more than a little stirred up since he'd arrived at the ranch. He might not trust her completely, but that didn't stop his desire for her.

"If I didn't know better I'd say you've been avoiding me." He moved under the protection of the shade tree. It didn't help cool him off.

Her eyes narrowed. "And why would I do that?"

Unable to resist her, he leaned forward. "Because of this…" His mouth covered hers and she drew back as she gave a weak gasp. Before she could work up a stronger protest, he brushed her hat off and thrust his fingers into her hair. He fit his lips to hers, his body to her body and kissed her with all the unfulfilled need that had built up for days.

When she moaned and took his tongue into her mouth, he almost blew apart. He wrapped her in his arms and reveled in the feel of her breasts against his chest. She trembled as her hands moved over his chest. Finally he broke off the kiss.

Damn. He gulped in air. "I've thought about doing that since the morning after your accident."

"So you followed me out here?" She stepped out of his embrace, grabbed her hat and put it back on her head.

"Yeah…I followed you because I wanted to see you." He grinned. "And from the way you greeted me, I think it's mutual."

Her gaze darted away. She didn't seem too happy to see him. "We can't always go with our… urges."

"Going with urges works for me."

She blew out a breath. "Not when there are far too many other things we need to think about right now."

He didn't like the fact that she'd been the one to put a halt to this. He raised his hands in surrender. "Fine. Not a problem. I'll back off."

Jack knew she had every right to be leery of a personal relationship, especially with an ex-cop from Seattle. Then why did he feel this need to convince her otherwise? Worse, why did he want their situation to be different? "I guess we have a few strikes against us."

"Yeah, just a few." She glanced away. "And in the end someone always gets hurt. So we need to stop this before anything starts."

He nodded in agreement, but he knew that it was already too late. He was way beyond start.

It was the right thing to do, Willow thought as she walked away from Jack. She climbed on Dakota and headed back to the house. She'd started to tell him about Dean's phone call, but she'd stopped herself.

What if Jack couldn't help Dean? And what if her brother did need a few days to find the guilty person?

Willow dug her heels into Dakota and the horse took off in a gallop across the meadow. Before she reached the barn, Willow detoured toward a large structure that doubled as an assembly and mess hall for the kids. She climbed down, tied the horse to the post and walked through the double doors.

Inside, the place was buzzing with activity. The long tables with matching benches were arranged in perfect rows, ready for tomorrow's festivities.

In the kitchen she found boxes of frozen food being placed into the large side-by-side freezers and canned goods lined the stainless steel counters.

Willow went around the center aisle to find Trevor. He was talking to the camp's cook, Maggie. After he finished their business, he walked to Willow and escorted her out of the crowded kitchen.

"How's it going?" she asked.

"Not bad." He pushed his cowboy hat back, exposing his wheat-colored hair. "The last of the food is being put away. Three of the counselors just arrived and are settling in." He released a breath. "Gina is helping with your mom. Seems Molly has worked her magic and got enough people to volunteer to help out with the filming."

"Really? She wasn't sure when I left this morning."

He nodded. "A skeleton crew will be here next weekend."

"Now we just need to get the kids enthusiastic, especially the boys."

He grinned. "I think Molly will be able to convince them, especially when they get into costume."

Willow was excited, too. "I'm glad I'm not in charge of the project. I just don't want it to be too much for Mom."

"This project seems to be the first thing she's gotten interested in since Matt died," Trevor said. "Your dad left a hole in all our lives, but he would want us to move on. And Molly is still young. She needs to make a life…without Matt."

Willow studied her friend. Trevor Adams was a good-looking man. Their fathers had been best friends, and there had been some hope their children would grow up and maybe marry.

"You know Dad loved you like a son."

Trevor smiled. "I thought a lot of him, too. Too bad his daughter didn't want to bring me into the family legally. You broke my heart, Willow."

It had been an ongoing joke over the years, since she'd brushed off Trevor's teenage advances.

Willow smacked his arm. "Yeah, I broke your heart

for about all of two weeks until you discovered Jessica Mullen."

"Well, she was every sixteen-year-old boy's fantasy." He sighed. "And I have such great memories."

"I just bet you do," Willow said. "Boy, am I glad you outgrew that behavior. And now, you've found someone nice."

He gave her a questioning look. "And who would that be?"

"You don't honestly think that you and Gina are fooling anyone. You're crazy about her."

He finally relented. "Yeah, I am. And I never wanted to hide my feelings for her. It's Gina who seems to think she isn't right for me. Her family is from East L.A., and her brother has been in trouble with the law."

Willow knew about Gina's family already. "I hope you convinced her that doesn't matter."

"I'm working on it." He sobered. "I love her."

She hugged him. "I'm so happy for you."

"Thanks." He pulled back and his gaze met hers. "But until I can convince Gina, she wants to keep our relationship quiet." Trevor studied her for a long time. "What about you, Willow? It's easy to see something's happening between you and Sullivan."

She shook her head. "Given the situation…it would be crazy to start anything. It's important I stay loyal to Dean."

Trevor remained quiet, and then said, "So little brother has put you in the middle again. As I recall you used to try to buffer things between him and Matt."

"Dean is family. He needs our support."

"Dean's a big boy, Willow. He needs to handle his own mistakes."

"You think Dean took the money, don't you?"

Trevor closed his eyes briefly. "I didn't say that. Only that everyone has always run to rescue Dean. Maybe you should wait until he asks for help."

"What if he didn't do it, Trevor? He said he was set up."

Trevor frowned. "You talked with Dean?"

Willow glanced around to see if anyone could hear them. "He called me less than an hour ago."

"Did you tell Jack?"

She shook her head.

Trevor turned away, and then swung back to her. "Willow, you're playing with fire here. Dean is in big trouble. If you help him, you could be an accessory to a crime."

"I didn't know what else to do. He only asked for two days. Two days to check out the person who really stole the money."

He started to speak, then shut his mouth. "Okay. Okay. I hope you know what you're doing...."

She didn't. She was caught in this mess. "All I want to do is protect my family." She studied her friend for a long time. "Two days, then I'll go to Jack."

Trevor nodded. "I think he's your best bet."

"Since when have you become a Jack Sullivan fan?"

He shrugged. "Once you get to know him, he seems like an okay guy. He's doing a good job here. He's worked hard this past week."

"We all have. And we need to remember the camp

comes first." She had to push any personal problems aside for now. "It's almost zero hour."

Trevor glanced at his watch. "Yep. In about… sixteen hours there will be a herd of kids running around here."

Willow glanced around. "What else needs to be done?"

"I think we're pretty much finished. Molly is going over the first week's agenda, and organizing the personnel for each activity."

"Then let's take tonight off and all go out for pizza," she said. "Whatever needs to be done, will work itself out."

Willow wanted to stop thinking for a while, about her brother's troubles, about the success of the summer camp. Mostly she didn't want to think about what would happen if Jack discovered she'd kept information from him.

She'd broken their agreement and all she could think about was how much she wanted it to be Sunday, and for Dean to call her back. There was no guarantee of anything. She could lose either way.

The next morning, the noise level was nearly deafening as Jack glanced around at the herd of kids. They'd all been checked in and assigned their cabins. Now, they were filing into the hall along with the counselors for the camp orientation.

It had brought back a lot of memories for him, both good and bad. As a kid, Jack had hated leaving his friends to go off to a stupid camp, but it also had hooked him up with Mike. The neighborhood cop had been the one who had suggested sending him in the first place. In the end they'd bonded and their close friendship began.

"Hey, man? Who do I talk to to get out of here?"

Jack glanced down to see a boy about nine or ten with dark blond hair hanging in his eyes, and a whole lot of attitude.

"You haven't even given camp a chance yet…" He glanced at the name tag. "Curtis."

"It's C.W."

"Okay, C.W. Why not wait until you spend a little time here before you pack it in?"

"Why? I don't want to ride a stupid horse, or sing lame camp songs."

"There are a lot of other things to do. Boating, fishing…" Jack stopped. It did sound lame to a city kid.

The boy glared. "I wasn't allowed to bring my skateboard."

Jack smiled. "No, it's a little hard to ride a skateboard in the pasture. Maybe you should give horseback riding a chance."

The boy tossed him an unimpressed look. "I didn't want to come in the first place. My mom just wants to spend time with her old man, without her kid gettin' in the way." The boy turned away so Jack wouldn't see him fighting tears. "Not a problem, I can crash at my friends' house. Just let me go back on the next bus."

Jack looked over the boy in the faded T-shirt and holey sneakers. He knew what it was like to be on his own, when no one cared if he came home or not.

"How about we make a deal? You give the camp two days and after that if you still want to go home… come see me."

C.W.'s eyes narrowed. "You're lyin.' "

Jack stared at him. "Two days, C.W. But you have to

participate in the activities." He had no business promising the boy anything, but too late, he was involved now. He reached out his hand for the boy to shake.

The kid ignored it. "Two days, mister." He turned and went back to his assigned seat.

"That went well," Jack murmured as he looked around and caught sight of Willow. She was busy with a group of girls, very excited girls. Except for one. The small child looked about ten.

Willow leaned down and wiped tears from the girl's cheeks. All the time, she kept talking and soothing the kid until they were both smiling. Then Willow took her small charge by the hand, and together, they walked to one of the young female counselors. After introductions, the child was left in the other woman's care.

Jack's chest tightened, fighting his own yearning for Willow's touch. A touch he knew could ignite him instantly. The thought of her kisses caused an ache throughout his body. She made him want what he never had with another woman. In the past every time he'd reached for someone, they left him. When he got old enough, he made sure he was the one to leave.

And he always walked away first.

As if Willow sensed him watching her, she turned and smiled. Desire rocked him to the core as he struggled to gather air in his lungs. Her smile was another thing he loved about her.

Whoa… He frowned. Where had that come from? He wanted Willow Kingsley, admired her and definitely thought she was beautiful…but that was as far as it could go.

Jack managed a nod as she went to the front of the room and stood at the microphone.

"Hello, boys and girls. Welcome to Kingsley's Kids Camp."

The rest of the conversation faded away as Jack walked out of the building and toward the shade trees. He drew a breath, then another. When had he lost his objectivity on this case?

Worse, she'd made him forget why he was even here. That left him no choice; he had to get out… and soon.

During most of the day's activities, Willow found herself looking for Jack. Not that he'd been assigned any activities, but she hadn't seen him since that morning's orientation. Finally it was nine o'clock and all campers were bedded down for the night… she hoped.

And she had survived the first day.

Willow headed for the house, resigned that Jack had other things to do. Besides, it was a bad idea to look for him, at least until Dean called her back.

She only prayed that her brother had good news she could relay to Jack. She hated lying to him.

Willow walked across the deserted campground when she heard feminine laughter. Suspicious that it was some of the kids, she went to investigate. In the shadows of the floodlights beside a cabin, she found one of the counselors. The pretty brunette, Kristin Metzger. Just out of college, she was eager to work with kids. Seemed she was eager to get up close and personal with Jack, too.

"Excuse me. I thought some kids were here…."

Willow's chest tightened, making her sound a little breathless.

"Sorry, Willow," Kristin said. "I just came out to check on some scratching noises and Jack said he'd help me."

Jack didn't look embarrassed about the situation. "I didn't think we needed a half-dozen girls screaming over a field mouse."

Willow couldn't look at him. "I'll have Larry set out traps under the cabins tomorrow." She directed her suggestion to Kristin. "You probably should get back to the girls. I'll have two of the hands patrol the area."

Kristin nodded and smiled at Jack. "Thanks for the help." The counselor walked across to the cabin and went inside.

"I didn't know you were on duty tonight."

Jack could sense that Willow wasn't happy at finding him roaming around camp. "I'm not. I was just a little restless and I thought I'd help out."

She glared at him. "You weren't given enough to do today to exhaust you?"

They started walking in the direction of the main house. "If you must know, I was checking on one of the kids," he told her.

"And you just happened to run into Kristin."

He studied her in the moonlight. "Yeah. That's exactly what happened."

"Well, if you want to get all cozy with her, you're going to have to wait until camp ends."

"Wait a minute here." He stopped her. "I'm too old to sneak around with a camp counselor. Just because you're jealous—"

"Jealous," she huffed. "In your dreams, Sullivan."

Jack found he enjoyed her discomfort. "You sure had me fooled. But just remember who called a halt to things yesterday."

"You come here accusing my brother of something illegal and you expect me to welcome you with open arms?"

"Come on, Willow, we said we'd be honest with each other. And I think you're lying…to both of us."

The next morning, Willow hurried into the mess hall just as the last group of kids took their seats. Great. The first official day of camp and she'd overslept.

She grabbed a tray and got in line for breakfast. Scanning the room, she looked for her mother and found her with Trevor. She didn't dare look for Jack. After what he said last night, she didn't want to give him any more ammunition.

She needed to keep her focus on the camp. First thing this morning was horseback riding. She knew Jack was on the schedule to work with a group of the younger boys, and she was working with the younger girls.

So they would be together. She could handle that.

She sat down across from her mother, alongside Trevor.

"I'm sorry," Molly said. "I should have made sure you were awake before I left. But it was so early I wanted you to sleep as long as possible."

"I guess I hit the snooze alarm a few too many times. I'm hoping the coffee will wake me up."

Her mother looked concerned. "You worked so hard already, Willow, maybe you should take it easy today."

She took a sip from her mug. "No way. I'm looking forward to being with the kids today."

"Well, just don't overdo. I'm looking forward to using your creative expertise when we begin the movie filming."

She smiled, remembering when she worked with her father. "It seems like so long ago."

Her mother smiled at her. "You better not have forgotten too much or I'm in trouble. Most of the crew is coming because you're involved. They also remember your work with Matt."

Willow set her fork down. "Mom, this is your project."

"Oh, I know I can get the kids to learn their lines, but you know a lot about what goes on behind the camera."

"I hope the campers are as excited as you are."

Molly's smile brightened. "Well, I'm going to dangle a carrot at them. Trevor offered to do some stunts."

Willow broke into laughter. "You are so bad. These kids don't have a chance."

"We want to have some fun. You know most of them just have big attitudes."

"Just remember, Molly, it's been a while since I ended my career as a stuntman."

"I know." Molly patted his hand. "Oh, I can't wait to tell everyone." She looked at Willow. "Would you mind if I make the announcements."

"Be my guest," Willow told her.

Molly got up from her seat and started for the podium at the front of the room. Something caught Willow's attention and she looked toward the door to see Jack walk in. If people didn't know, they'd think he'd been born on a ranch. In jeans and chambray shirt, his gait slow and deliberate as he crossed the room. He removed his hat and hung it on a hook. Jack stopped by a table of girls, Kristin's girls. By the time he left, all the girls were giggling, and the counselor's gaze followed him. He got his breakfast, then carried his tray to a boys' table and sat down. The young boy beside him didn't seem all that happy to have him there, but Jack kept talking to him.

Then all attention went to Molly Reynolds at the front of the room. "Hello, boys and girls. My name is Molly and we have a new activity this year at camp." Her smiled widened. "How do you all feel about making a real western movie?"

"I don't want to get on any horse," C.W. told Jack.

Jack stood beside Cisco, holding his reins at the ramp. Several of the other kids had already mounted and were riding around the corral.

"I thought we made a deal, C.W. You have to give camp a chance."

The boy studied the large animal. "I don't like horses."

"How do you know? You told me you've never been around any. I hadn't, either, until I went to camp." When the boy didn't move, Jack led Cisco from the ramp so the next camper could get on his horse.

After he tied the animal to the fence, he came and took C.W. by the arm. "Look, it's okay to admit you're afraid."

"I'm not afraid," the boy denied.

"Okay. Look at it this way. If you ride a skateboard, you've got to have great balance…and guts. You'd be a good rider."

C.W. glared at him. "What if I suck at it? And everyone laughs at me?"

Jack glanced around at the kids sitting in the saddles, some holding on for dear life, others bouncing up and down as they were being led around the corral.

"I don't think anyone is going to laugh." He leaned toward his stubborn student. "And I'm going to make a bet that you'll learn the basics of riding within the hour. And you could be the best rider here."

C.W. sized him up. "Yeah? I could do it, if I wanted to."

"Look, I'll be right beside you. I won't leave you." He paused. "How about we go meet Cisco? Here, I've even got a carrot you can give him."

Jack went over all the safety rules of being around a horse. Though C.W. still wasn't overfriendly with the animal, he put on the helmet and let Jack help him into the saddle. After adjusting the stirrups, Jack took Cisco's reins and they began the journey around the pen.

They'd gone around once when Jack looked at his rider to see the joy on his face. He felt his chest constrict at the simple expression.

"Hey, C.W., look at you go," a female voice said.

Jack turned to see Willow sitting on the fence watching them. She had on her usual jeans and western shirt. Her hair was braided, and a hat cocked low on her head. She was grinning as they walked toward her.

C.W. was affected by her, too. The boy sat a little straighter in the saddle. "Jack said because I skateboard, I have good balance."

She gave him a close examination. "You sure do. And you have a good horse with Cisco. I used to ride him."

She jumped down from the fence, moved to C.W.'s side and began walking along with them. Jack wasn't offended. He'd use any help to get the boy to respond. And damn, who wouldn't respond to Willow Kingsley?

"How come you don't ride him anymore?" C.W. asked.

"Because I ride Dakota now. He belonged to my dad…. He died a few years ago."

"Oh," the boy said as he continued to watch Willow.

Jack slowed the horse to a stop as she talked with the boy.

"Dakota was lonely for my dad and I was lonely, so we just started riding together." She blinked and patted Cisco's rump. "It's good for both of us. And Cisco gets ridden by the ranch hands and you kids." She smiled. "So he's happy, too."

C.W. looked at her. "I'm sorry about your dad," he murmured. "I don't have a dad anymore, either."

Willow came closer. "I'm sorry about your dad, too, C.W." She placed her hand on the horse's neck. "Maybe you can do what I do…and ride. That always makes me feel better."

"Really?"

She nodded. "So you take care of Cisco."

"I will," he promised. "Hey, Willow, can I ride him again?"

"Sure." She turned back to the horse. "Hey, Cisco, do you want C.W. to ride you every day?"

The horse bobbed his head up and down, then whinnied. They all laughed. "I think that means yes." She patted the boy's leg, and started off.

Jack just watched her go. Well, he'd be damned.

Willow had managed to do in minutes what he'd been trying to do for two days.

As if she'd read his mind, she turned that smile on him. He was in big trouble.

CHAPTER SEVEN

IN A LITTLE OVER twenty-four hours, Jack had created a monster.

C.W. hadn't left his side the entire morning as they went from one activity to the next. Even though Jack found he had a good time, trying to keep up with the kids exhausted him.

Jack finally got a break at lunch, and he headed to the assigned table for the ranch hands. Of course, when he walked by Kristin's group, all her girls called and waved to him. And he got a special smile from the counselor herself.

He reached his seat and Larry let him have it. "Oh, Jack," he mimicked. "Thank you for saving us from the big old mouse last night." All the men laughed.

"Very funny," he said. "You guys are just jealous."

"Well, it's my turn tonight to guard her cabin," Jason said. He was one of the younger college students who'd taken the job for the camp. "I want Kristin to notice me, too."

Trevor arrived. "Remember, no fraternizing with the counselors," he said as he took his seat. "Not to say you couldn't get her phone number and call her after camp is over."

Jason smiled, then quickly finished his sandwich. "I better go. I've got a group of riders this afternoon." He stood, took his tray and walked to the kitchen. Soon, one by one, the rest of the men went back to work.

Jack looked around the hall but didn't see Willow.

"She's not here," Trevor said.

There wasn't any point to acting as if he didn't know who Trevor was talking about. "Is she okay?"

Trevor took a bite of his sloppy joe sandwich and swallowed. "She went up to Liberty to check out the equipment in the storage area."

"Why her? I thought Molly was heading this project."

"She is, but Willow used to be the production manager on her father's western series. She knows where everything is. She went to take inventory."

Jack glanced across the room to see Molly make her way around the hall. "She went alone?"

Trevor smiled. "Don't worry, Willow knows how to take care of herself. Besides, you get too protective, she gets irritated."

"There's reason to be protective," Jack said. "You know what happened the last time we went up there."

The foreman smiled. "I think it's safe to say she'll stay away from the jail."

"I still don't think she should be up there by herself."

"Then maybe you should be the one to go tell her," Trevor suggested. He reached into his pocket and pulled out a set of keys. "Take the Jeep." He pointed toward the west. "Past the barn there's a dirt road, it'll lead you right to her. A lot faster, too."

"Why are you sending me?"

Trevor studied him for a few seconds, and said, "I know you'll look out for her. She hasn't had many guys in her past who have, and that includes Dean."

Wonderful memories flooded through Willow as she walked into the production office. The room on the main floor of the saloon still had publicity pictures of her dad on the walls. He'd been so handsome with thick, dark brown hair and piercing whiskey-colored eyes. No wonder the women couldn't resist him…including her mother.

Willow remembered the loving husband and father. She knew how much her dad wanted a family. His horrible childhood back in Oklahoma had caused him to run away at sixteen. Eventually he worked his way to California. His good looks got him to Hollywood and into the movies.

Her thoughts turned to Jack. The man reminded her of her father in so many ways. They both had those dark, good looks. Their similar childhoods. Matt had one true friend in stunt double Sligh Adams. With Jack, it had been his partner on the police force, Mike. Both men were loyal, and didn't trust easily.

Would Jack ever let anyone else get close? Had he risked giving his heart to another woman? She sighed and walked to the desk, knowing she should stay away from him. Any day now, he could leave…no doubt taking her heart.

Worse, he could destroy her family, too.

She'd already been put in the middle between Dean and Jack. Her brother was supposed to call her today. He hadn't. Of course it wasn't the first promise Dean had broken. But this time, the problem didn't just involve her brother. She and her mother had a big stake in the outcome of this situation at Walsh Enterprises.

Willow picked up the receiver from the landline phone on the desk and heard a dial tone. Her mother had gotten it turned back on. She immediately punched in the Seattle number she'd been calling for the past week.

This time someone picked up, but he or she remained silent. "Heather…Dean…It's Willow." She waited, feeling her heart pounding. Nothing. "Look, someone better talk to me and fast, because I'm tired of being left in the dark. Dean, I can't help you if you don't let me."

"Willow…" her brother finally said.

She sighed. "Dean, I've been worried about you. Why didn't you call me?"

"What's the use? I didn't have any news to tell you, because the guy won't talk to me."

"What do you mean? Who are you talking about?"

"My supervisor, Brad Lansing. I know he did this to me. He took my idea and used it against me."

"Are you saying that your boss stole the money?"

There was a long pause. "Yeah, but he made it look like I did it. And I was dumb enough to believe he was going to help me."

Her head was spinning with unfamiliar details. "Dean, are you still in Seattle?"

"No. I had to leave."

"Are you close by?"

"Yeah, I'm in L.A."

Willow didn't know if she should be relieved or not. Her brother was in trouble…and she only had one way to go.

She heard something and turned to look over her shoulder to find Jack standing in the doorway. Her pulse began to race when she saw the look on his face. He'd heard the conversation.

Willow needed to deal with Dean first. "Look, I've got to go, but I will call you back. So you answer the phone."

"Is someone there?"

"I'll talk to you later. Bye." She hung up and stood to face Jack. His calm rattled her more than if he'd started yelling at her.

"How long have you been in contact with your brother?"

She couldn't lie anymore, not if she wanted his help. And she did. "Dean called me Friday and asked for two days because he had a lead on who set him up. I was going to tell you."

His nostrils flared. "And I'm supposed to believe you?"

"I would have told you that same day, but I had no information to give you. I didn't know where Dean was. I swear."

"Again, why should I believe you?"

"It's true. He only said that someone had set him up."

"And without Dean…I can't get any proof."

"He's here in L.A."

"Where?" Jack asked.

"I didn't get the address, but I'll call him back and find out."

"Willow, when are you going to realize that your

brother is using you?" He stared at her for a long time. "I'm out of here." He turned and strode out of the room.

Suddenly Willow felt abandoned. She hadn't realized how she'd relied on Jack. "Jack, wait." She ran through the saloon and caught him at the Jeep. "I'll call Dean back, and you can talk to him."

He ignored her as he climbed into the driver's seat. "You had plenty of time to talk to me last Friday." He glared at her. "I hate being lied to."

"I'm sorry." She touched him on the arm. "I'll find Dean, I promise."

He started the engine. "And we both know how good you are at keeping promises. I'm through playing ranch hand. I'm going back to Seattle." His gaze met hers once more. "And stop looking at me with those eyes, thinking you can have your way. I won't be a fool a second time."

He put the vehicle in gear and shot off, kicking up dust in his path and finally disappeared down the road.

Willow had never felt so alone, and she had no one to blame but herself.

Jack got back to the ranch in record time. He couldn't think about anything other than he'd been played for a fool. He'd let the woman get to him.

Well, his time here was over. He needed to get back to Seattle and pick up the pieces. If he hadn't screwed up this job already. Maybe it was time to get the police involved, and let them handle Kingsley.

He parked the Jeep behind the barn and started for the bunkhouse when he heard his name. He turned and saw C.W. running toward him, something in his hand.

"Hey, Jack. Where you been?"

"I had to drive up to Liberty."

The boy's eyes widened. "For the movie we're going to make?"

Jack made himself smile. "That's the one."

"Miss Molly said I should try out." He shrugged. "It's probably a lame idea. The older kids will probably get all the cool parts, but she said maybe I could play like a deputy or one of the ranch hands who get to ride a horse and bring the herd of cattle into the town." The boy looked up at him. "What do you think?"

It ate at his gut, how the boy looked to him for guidance. "It's not what I think that matters. It could be fun."

"Trevor is going to teach some kids how to move cattle. They're using real steers. That's cool. So I need to practice riding Cisco." The boy's dark eyes raised to meet Jack's. "Will you help me?"

C.W.'s enthusiasm tore at him. The kid asked for so little, and now, he had to disappoint him, too. And he knew how that felt. "Hey, that's great. And I want nothing more than to help you, but I have to go back to Seattle in the morning. Something came up."

The look on C.W.'s face told him everything. "I don't want to be in the stupid show anyway. Here, I made you this dumb belt."

The boy started to run off, but Jack stopped him. "Hey, C.W., this is a great belt. Thanks. And I have a job to do in Seattle, that's the reason I have to go."

The boy swiped his hand under his nose. "You think I care? Well, I don't. This is just a dumb camp." Before Jack could say any more, the boy took off.

Jack stared down at the strip of leather in his hand. The name Jack was tooled across the back in crooked letters.

Trevor appeared. "C.W. worked hard on that today. What's he so upset about?"

Jack looked at the foreman. "He just learned a hard lesson. For some of us, it takes longer."

That evening, Jack propped the pillow behind his head, trying to get comfortable on the lumpy motel mattress. He tried to concentrate on the television show, but he wasn't interested. Well, he'd be leaving soon so his accommodations didn't matter.

Tomorrow, he'd be gone. He had a reservation on a flight to Seattle at noon. He could forget about the Wandering Creek Ranch and Willow Kingsley. It hadn't been worth his time to come here.

He'd talked with Stan just thirty minutes ago, but hadn't told him Willow had been in contact with her brother. Maybe it was stupid, and he definitely wasn't thinking with his brain, but he still wanted to check out Lansing first.

A while back, Jack recalled meeting the executive assistant. He remembered Stan mentioning how much he liked Lansing, also how much he wished Brad and Heather would get together. It didn't seem that she ever returned those feelings. So the CEO's daughter was on the top of his list for some information. So far, nothing in this puzzle had come together, yet.

Jack heard a faint knocking sound. He got up and opened the door to find Willow, standing there in the cool night. "What are you doing here?"

He saw the hurt on her face and regretted his words.

"Trevor told me where to find you," she said. "I'm probably being foolish, but I think I deserved better than you just leaving."

"I told you I had to return to Seattle. Besides, we said everything. So go back to your campers."

"I know what my job is, as you know yours." She folded her arms. "So, you burst into my life, and turn everything upside down, then you take off when things don't go your way." Those rich blue eyes locked on his, daring him to deny it.

"Sorry, it's the hazards of this job."

"That doesn't mean I have to like it," she told him.

"You were the one who withheld information."

"There was nothing to tell you," she argued.

Before he could answer, someone came out of the room next to them. He gripped her by the arm and pulled her inside. Shutting the door, she leaned against it. The space between them was barely inches, but he couldn't seem to move away from her. He inhaled her fruity scent, her soft hair. She was intoxicating.

"Aren't you worried about photographers following you here?" he asked.

"Not as much as I want to know why you left so suddenly. Don't you want to talk to my brother?"

"I'd say hanging around to wait for that to happen isn't worth my time," he lied.

She glanced away momentarily. "That's all you can say about the past ten days?" Her azure glance met his.

He knew she wasn't only talking about his job. He'd made the mistake of letting her get to him. He could lose much more than just this job if he let her get too close.

"What do you want to hear, Willow? That you got to me, that I fell for you?" He shook his head, denying his true feelings. "It's part of the job. I do what it takes to get the info I need."

"I think you're lying. I got to you, as you got to me." She swallowed. "I messed up, Jack. I should have told you about Dean."

He turned away.

When she touched his arm, he turned back around. "I know I need you, more than you need me. Please, Jack, will you help me prove my brother's innocence?"

He blinked. "How can I? He's not even around to help explain what happened."

"Yes, he is." She opened the door and waved her hand. A car door opened and a young man about six feet tall walked toward them. He had on a hooded sweatshirt but blond hair fell across his forehead. His eyes were a golden brown. Jack definitely saw the family resemblance.

Willow pulled him inside the room and closed the door. "Jack, my brother, Dean. Dean, Jack Sullivan."

Dean nodded. The kid looked to be in his mid-twenties, and Jack doubted he even shaved regularly.

"Willow said you're good at your job." He stole a glance at his sister. "She also said maybe you'd help me."

"Not if you stole from Walsh."

"Man, do you think I'd be hanging here if I stole a million dollars? I'd be on an island somewhere."

"Not necessarily," Jack said. "Not if you think you'd get away with it."

"I'm not stupid, Mr. Sullivan."

"Jack," he corrected.

"All right, Jack." Dean repeated the name as he and Willow went to stand by a small table. "The one claim to fame I have—besides my famous parents—is that I scored 1600 on my SAT tests. And I'm a computer wiz. I was hired at Walsh Enterprises as a computer programmer, but I wanted to move up in the company. I met Heather and we started dating. For a while I'd been working on developing protocols to protect against online theft."

"So you tried it out?"

"No." Dean glanced at his sister. "I did it by the book. I approached Lansing with the idea for security protocols that would limit access to sensitive data. Brad was impressed and said he would present it to Mr. Walsh. That was last month. Two and a half weeks ago, I saw all the audit guys hanging around, asking questions.

"It was Heather who told me what was going on. When I talked to Brad, he just played innocent, denying anything and everything about my ideas."

Dean stood and began to walk around the room. "You've got to believe me, I didn't steal any money. I don't have the ID access to get into that sensitive system. Brad does. He could have used my ID and password."

"Why should I believe you?" Jack asked. "I mean, Lansing has three years with the company."

"If I was going to steal, I'd do a better job of it. At least I wouldn't point the finger at myself."

Jack didn't know what to think. But this story seemed so far-fetched it could possibly be true.

"Why would Lansing single you out?"

"I think because of Heather Walsh. They used to date a while back. Heather said Brad was pretty persistent about wanting to marry her. She broke it off, but he's never left her alone."

"So you're saying Lansing did all this for love."

"Or greed. I don't know which." Dean shook his head. "I just know I didn't steal any money."

Willow had remained quiet until now. "Jack, could you at least test this theory? Dean does raise some good questions."

Jack had a lot of questions, too. He'd grill the kid more, later. "Okay, if I follow this lead, you'll have to do everything I say."

Dean nodded. "Sure."

"I know computers, but you know your program so I'll need you with me." He took out his cell phone and pressed the programmed number for the airlines. When he finally got a person, he requested, "I need two tickets from LAX to Seattle-Tacoma International."

Willow went to him. "Make it three tickets."

Oh, no. The last thing Jack wanted was for her to go along. That made this all too personal. He didn't do personal.

"I'll stay out of the way, I promise," she told him. "But I have to be there."

"What about the camp? Your mother needs you."

"I can get her some help for a few days," she told him.

"This could all blow up in our faces."

She reached for her brother. "Then all the more reason I should be there."

Jack knew she was relying on him to pull this off. What if he couldn't? He wasn't anybody's hero... hadn't been for a long, long time.

In the morning, Willow was dropped off by one of the ranch hands. She had an overnight bag and some fresh clothes for Dean who'd spent the night in Jack's extra bed in the motel room.

The short plane ride wasn't memorable. There was only minimal conversation. What was there to say? This was business.

Since Jack had to leave his car at LAX, he got a rental when they arrived in Seattle, then drove them to his house in Green Lake. He told himself he needed room to work with Dean before they went into the office and talked with Walsh Enterprises' network people.

Willow had to hold back a gasp when Jack pulled in the driveway of a small Tudor-style house. The brick-and-wood structure was painted cream with chocolate-brown trim. There were several plants that edged a well-manicured lawn. To say she was surprised was an understatement.

"You live here?" she asked.

"Don't look so surprised," he told her. "I have to live somewhere. I can't sleep in my car all the time."

He climbed out, and grabbed the bags from the trunk. Dean took charge of his own along with his sister's. They went to the porch.

Willow found she was excited to see Jack's home. He'd hidden so much from her. If maybe she could see inside the man... She'd what? Love him less?

Inside, a scattering of rugs on the hardwood floors led into the living room with a small fireplace and a long black leather sofa and a recliner. Again there were plants.

Jack pointed toward the kitchen. "Dean, you can sleep in the game room in the basement. There's a pullout sofa bed and a bath."

"Thanks, man. I appreciate it."

Jack glanced at her. "You can take my room upstairs."

"No, I can't do that."

"There's a second bedroom that's my office. I'll sleep on the sofa."

She shook her head. "I'll sleep on the sofa."

"This isn't up for negotiation, Willow." He looked at Dean. "Get settled in and I'll call you when I'm ready to work. We have a lot of things to go over before I talk to Walsh."

Dean nodded and headed to the basement door that led downstairs to his room.

Willow followed Jack up to the second floor. The hardwood creaked as they made their way along the hall. He stopped at the second bedroom. "It's not much on decor, but it's comfortable."

Willow walked into the medium-sized room that displayed a large bed as the centerpiece. The dark blues and brown let you know this was a man's room. She walked to the dresser and the photos. She picked up one of Jack in a police uniform, alongside an older man with short gray hair and a contagious smile. The name on the badge read, M. Gerick.

Mike. Jack's partner. She felt tears prickle in her eyes. The love between the two was obvious. She glanced at another picture, this one of Mike and a middle-aged woman. His wife?

"That's Mike and his wife, Carol. She's the one who keeps me in plants."

"Does she live close by?"

"Two blocks over. I can't seem to keep her out of my yard." He fought a smile. "Said it helps her mental health to work in the soil."

"She does a good job."

He nodded. "She's been lonely without Mike."

Jack stood by Willow as they studied the picture. They were so close she could smell his soap and the man himself. Intoxicating.

"They were married for over thirty years," he said.

"Any children?"

Jack shook his head. "No. Carol said they weren't blessed with their own. Mike said they liked to pick up strays."

"Weren't you lucky," Willow told him, "to have people like the Gericks in your life."

"You mean for a kid who was a bother to his mom and didn't know his father?" Suddenly Jack's expression changed. "I better get busy with some food. A couple of pizzas would be easiest. I'll go to the store and pick up some staples. Keep your brother here and don't let him call Heather until this mess is straightened out." He started out of the room.

"Jack," she called, causing him to stop and look over his shoulder. As much as she'd tried to keep him at arm's length, she wanted nothing more at this moment than to be held by him. "Thank you again."

He shrugged. "It's my job, Willow, it's just my job."

"You could have dumped Dean in Walsh's lap," she said.

"There are too many unanswered questions." He pinned her with a stare. "That's the reason I needed to talk to your brother. I still need to talk him. There are a lot more questions that need answers."

Her spirits soared. He did believe in Dean. "Why is it so hard for you to accept that you're a nice guy?"

He stood there awhile. "Maybe at one time I was, but that guy has been gone a long time."

CHAPTER EIGHT

AFTER THEY ATE SUPPER, the guys disappeared upstairs to the office, leaving Willow alone.

She tried to keep her mind busy with other things. So she straightened the kitchen, all the while enjoying the fifties' decor. The yellow-and-green tiles that covered the counters, the older, but well-maintained appliances. Even the homey-style curtains that hung in the row of windows next to the small maple table with four captain's chairs appealed to her.

At about nine o'clock, Willow went up to her assigned room. Sitting on the bed, she took out her cell phone and called her mother to hear how things went that day at camp.

"Hi, Mom," she said when her mother answered.

"Oh, hi, honey. How is it going?"

"I'll know more tomorrow after Jack takes Dean into the office for a strategy meeting."

"How is Dean holding up?"

"Surprisingly well. He's with Jack, going over the possibilities of how Lansing got into Walsh's system."

There was a long pause, then her mother said, "We're lucky to have Jack helping us."

Willow wanted to second that. "I think he wants to get to the bottom of this mess, too."

After a long pause, her mother asked, "How are you doing?"

"Fine. I hated to leave you alone with the kids."

"It's not too bad. Except for some minor trouble with Curtis, things have been pretty quiet here."

"What happened with C.W.?" Willow knew how attached the boy had gotten to Jack.

"He got into a fight with one of the older boys." Molly sighed. "I think he was being teased about something. Anyway, Trevor handled it."

"Well, I'll be back tomorrow evening."

There was another pause.

"Is there something else, Mom?"

"No, I was just hoping Jack would be returning, too. I like him."

Willow didn't allow herself to wish for anything more than to exonerate Dean. As for Jack, he'd let her know that he didn't do relationships. "Mom, Jack has a home and a career…here."

"People relocate all the time."

"Mom. Don't play matchmaker, please. Jack Sullivan isn't the man for me," she lied.

"He's the perfect man for you. Don't try to deny it. And I know Jack has feelings for you, too."

Willow blinked at her tears. "Mom, he's made it perfectly clear what his feelings for me are. The only reason

I'm here is because I pressed the issue. He can't wait to get rid of me."

"That's because he's afraid to trust anyone, afraid he'll be hurt…again. Your father acted the same way with me. You just have to let Jack know you care about him."

But what if she reached out and he didn't want her? "I need to go."

"Okay, I'll stop," her mother promised. "Give Dean a kiss, and call tomorrow the minute you hear anything. I love you, Willow."

"I love you, too, Mom. Bye." She closed her phone, and lay back on the bed.

How did her life get so complicated? Two weeks ago, all she had on her mind was reopening the camp. Now, her brother was in serious trouble, and she was crazy in love with a man who couldn't wait to get her out of his life.

Was she brave enough to go after Jack, and let him know how she felt?

It was after midnight and Jack threw back the blanket and sat up. The damn sofa was too short to get comfortable. A bigger problem, he couldn't turn off his head. He'd sent Dean downstairs around eleven to get some sleep. If everything the kid told him was true, then the trail would lead to Lansing.

All Jack had to do was convince Walsh to let him talk with the network people. It was going to work, he told himself. Then he could close this case, send the Kingsleys home and move on to something else.

Not so easy to do. Not this time. Even with three

more jobs lined up to begin immediately, he knew he wouldn't be able to forget her.

Willow was going to be with him for longer. That was why he didn't want her here...in his house. After she went back to L.A., he'd still picture her in his kitchen, still inhale her fragrance in his bath, and worst of all, he'd still imagine her in his bed.

Damn. He stood and rubbed his hand over his face. He had to stop this. He pulled on a pair of sweats and grabbed his hooded sweatshirt. Pushing his arms into the sleeves, he started out of the room and into the dark hall. He took two steps then he ran into another body. Willow.

"Oh, Jack," she gasped. "You scared me."

He gripped her bare arms and his body immediately surged to life. "What are you doing up?"

"I need some water," she said, but didn't move back.

He couldn't seem to let go, either. "It's late, you should get some sleep."

"I can't sleep," she admitted. "What are you doing up?"

"I'm a little restless myself. Thought I'd go for a run."

The darkness cocooned them, making the small space even more intimate. "Oh."

He suddenly became aware of her hands against his chest. A slow burn began to move through him.

He sucked in a breath. "Willow." He tried to send a warning, but it wasn't heartfelt. "What are you doing?"

"If I have to explain, then I guess I'm not doing it right."

"Oh, babe, you're doing it right...too right." Her touch was killing him. "But it's wrong."

"Why is it wrong, Jack? Don't you want me?"

"I haven't made any secret that I've been attracted to you from the beginning."

He heard the catch in her breath.

"Is that what you want to hear, Willow? That I want you?"

"A girl still likes to hear these things."

He'd never let a woman get to him…not the way he had Willow. He could lose everything if she got close. If he gave in to his feelings and lost again…

"And that's all it's going to be. Just talk." No matter how much he wanted her. "Look, Willow, I'm trying to do the right thing here. It would never work between us. So you turn around and go back to bed." He took a step back so she could get by.

She just stood there. "What if it's just you who thinks it's the right thing to do? To ignore what's between us."

He shut his eyes, feeling the tremors of his slipping control. "I'm trying to protect you—"

"I'm a big girl," she interrupted. "I can take care of myself." She sounded so innocent.

"Not in my world you can't," he challenged. "I've seen too much…and it's made me cynical." He started to reach out for her, but stopped himself. "Oh, God, Willow, I don't want any of that to touch you."

She didn't move. "Are you talking about Mike?"

His chest tightened painfully. "Yeah. He was one of the good guys."

"So are you."

"The only good in me was because of Mike Gerick."

She took a step toward him. "That's not true. He

saw the good in you, or he never would have stayed in your life."

"My partner had this obsession with wanting to save lost souls." Hundreds of memories flooded Jack's head. "Mike used to say he didn't like to fail, so I'd better get my act together, because I was messing up his perfect record."

Jack couldn't help but laugh, but it didn't relieve his tension. The need to touch her was unbearable. He took her hand and pulled her into his dimly lit bedroom. Now, he could see her pretty face.

For the first time, he glanced down at her sleeping attire, a pink tank top and a pair of pajama bottoms. She looked far too sexy, and suddenly all thoughts of Mike began to fade. Temptation won out and he pulled her into his arms.

"Damn, I want you, Willow," he practically growled. "So much so that I can't remember my own name." He leaned in and nuzzled her neck, worked his way to her ear and whispered things he wanted to do to her.

She gasped, but didn't push him away. Jack raised his head to see a mix of innocence and hunger in her eyes.

"But that's all this can be, Willow. Tonight. Tomorrow, it's back to business. However the outcome with Walsh, you go home…and I stay here."

Without hesitation, she said, "Then stop wasting time talking." She moved her hand up his chest, ever so slowly…then slipped her fingers into his hair. She rose on her toes; her lips hovered just inches from his. "Make love to me, Jack."

His mouth closed over hers in a hungry kiss. This

time he groaned as she opened eagerly to receive his tongue. He wanted more…. He wanted to devour her.

Jack lifted her into his arms, crossed the room and stood her next to the bed. His hands went to her top, tugging the thin straps down, tugging the fabric away to expose her breasts. Her labored breathing teased his already overtaxed libido.

"You are so beautiful." He pulled her back into his arms and kissed her. Before it ended, they were lying on the bed.

Willow didn't want to think about how crazy this was. All she knew was that she was in love with a man who planned to walk out of her life. She had only a few hours to prove they belonged together…forever.

"You're pretty beautiful yourself."

That got her a cocky grin. Then he reached for the remote on the bed table and soft music filtered into the space. "That's a little better." He leaned down and kissed her, nibbling gently, tugging on her bottom lip. "But this is much better." He went back for more. Then his mouth roved down her neck to her breasts and sucked gently. She whimpered as his lips worked their magic along her flesh.

Willow put everything out of her mind but this man. If tonight was all she had, then she'd fill her senses with him…and only him.

The sound of the rain against the windowpane woke Willow. It was still dark out and she snuggled closer to get warm, encountering the hard naked body. Jack. All the sweet memories of their lovemaking came back in a rush. She smiled and placed a kiss again his gorgeous chest. The swirl of dark hair tickled her nose but she continued her journey.

Jack groaned as his arms wrapped around her and tugged her body on top of his. "I think I've died and gone to heaven."

"Not yet, but maybe if you're lucky," she breathed into the darkness. There was just a shadow of his head against the pillow. "Do you feel lucky?" She placed teasing kisses along his jaw and mouth as her body moved against his.

"Woman, you're killing me."

She went back and nipped at his lower lip. "You feel pretty alive to me."

She gasped when he flipped her on her back, pinning her to the mattress. Her heart raced in excitement. She couldn't see his face, but knew he was smiling.

"Let's see how you like the way I play the game," he whispered.

Then he lowered his head to her mouth and she soon was lost in his kiss. She closed her eyes and savored every touch, every caress that brought her body to life. She'd never been loved like this before.

She'd tuck away the night's memories because when tomorrow came and she woke up, this dream would end…forever.

Rare Seattle sunlight shone through the bedroom window. Willow squinted and memories of last night flooded her head. With a smile she turned to the other side of the bed. It was empty. There was a note. She opened the folded piece of paper.

Willow, You looked too tempting, so I decided it was best I go for a run. J.

"So I got to you, Jack Sullivan." She smiled as she headed for the shower.

Fifteen minutes later she was dressed in khaki pants and a light blue camp-style blouse. Downstairs in the kitchen, she poured a cup of coffee that Jack must have made before his run. After a few sips she went to the refrigerator and took out bacon and eggs. They all needed breakfast before their busy day.

Willow put strips of bacon in the microwave, then pulled down a bowl and began cracking eggs against the side. She was humming around the kitchen when suddenly there was a knock on the back door.

Willow went to answer it. She recognized the older woman on the stoop from the picture upstairs. Carol Gerick.

"Oh, my," the older woman gasped. "I'm sorry, I didn't realize…" She gripped the basket in her hands. "It's just Jack never…he never has…" She blinked. "I should go."

"Wait. Mrs. Gerick?" Willow reached for her. "Please, stay. Jack should be back soon."

The attractive sixty-something woman in her navy capris and red-checkered blouse looked fresh and sweet. "I don't want to intrude."

"You aren't." Willow knew that whatever happened last night didn't change the reality of today's events. "Jack was nice enough to help my brother. I'm Willow Kingsley and I'm here for moral support. Please, come in and stay. I know Jack will be happy to see you."

"Willow. What an unusual name," the older woman said as she came inside.

Willow smiled. "It's a family name."

The woman studied her. "It fits you. So, you're from around here?"

"No, the L.A. area. Hopefully, we'll be heading back today. I kind of left my mother in charge of sixty kids."

"Oh, my. That's a lot of kids."

Willow went back to the stove, and continued to break the eggs. "We run a children's summer camp at our ranch."

Suddenly the back door opened again. "I smell bacon cooking. Man, I'm hungry as a bear." Jack came in wearing a pair of sweatpants and a track T-shirt, revealing his wide shoulders and muscular arms.

Willow's body heated, seeing the glint in his eyes as he glanced at her. Then it quickly disappeared as he spotted Carol.

"Carol!" He swept her up into a big hug. "What a pleasant surprise."

Once on the ground the woman said, "I know it's a surprise, but I don't know how pleasant. I just brought over some blueberry muffins. I'm sorry, Jack, I didn't know you had…guests."

Willow stepped in. "I was explaining to Carol how you were helping Dean. And how I just tagged along."

Smiling, Carol glanced at both of them. She wasn't buying the story.

Jack checked his watch. "In fact, I better get a move on. Carol, stay for breakfast." He glanced at Willow. "Do I have time for a quick shower?"

She nodded, trying not to think about him being

naked and how much she wanted to join him. Their eyes met momentarily, but all too soon, he grabbed a mug of coffee and left to go upstairs.

"Jack's a great guy," Carol said, bringing Willow back to reality. "He probably works too hard, but so did my husband."

Willow opened the refrigerator and took out the gallon jug of orange juice. "Jack speaks highly of Mike."

"The feeling was mutual. Mike loved him like a son." She smiled and raised an eyebrow. "So, all this time that Jack's been in L.A., he's been at your ranch?"

"My parents' ranch. My dad started a summer camp before he died. Mom and I restarted it this year. Kingsley's Kids Camp."

Those hazel eyes widened. "Oh, goodness, your father was Matt Kingsley. And your mother is Molly Reynolds."

Willow smiled. "Yes, and yes."

Carol took out a skillet and placed it on the stove. "Matt was so handsome. Whenever one of his movies came out, I had to see it on the first day. Used to make Mike so jealous." She sighed dreamily.

Willow smiled as she poured the eggs into the hot pan. "I bet it was wonderful growing up there."

"It was good and bad," Willow said. "But my parents tried hard to make a normal life for us. My dad was the best. Not many men can live up to him."

"Spoken like a loving daughter."

She stirred the eggs and turned down the flame. "I've tried to be." Would her father approve of her loyalty? "I better see if my brother is up." She went to the stairs, but the basement door opened and Dean appeared dressed for the day.

"Great timing," she said. "Breakfast is ready."

He nodded, not looking too happy. "I'm not really hungry."

"Well, try to eat something, because it's going to be a long day."

Dean looked at Carol.

"Dean, this is Carol Gerick. Carol, my brother, Dean Kingsley."

"Hi, Dean. I'm Jack's neighbor and friend."

"It's nice to meet you, Carol." Dean turned to Willow. "I think I'll go wait in Jack's office."

Willow wanted to call her brother back, but knew this day would be rough on him. It had been rough on all the family.

She went to dish up the food just as Jack walked into the room. "Man, I'm hungry."

"Well, sit down," Carol said as she set her muffins on the table.

Willow tried to stay busy, and not look at the man she'd spent the night with. She had a feeling Carol already knew.

Breakfast was eaten quickly and the conversation was led by Carol asking questions mostly about camp. Soon the kitchen was cleaned up and Carol was on her way.

Alone at the table, Jack couldn't look at Willow. She'd already weakened his resolve. He'd told her last night that was all there could be between them. It was a lie. He'd gone for a run this morning, trying to push any thoughts of permanence out of his head. It didn't work. And he'd rushed back to spill his guts when Carol's appearance saved him.

The more the two women talked about the Kingsley family, the more he realized that he'd never fit into Willow's life. Any more than she'd fit into his.

"Are you going to freeze me out?"

Jack finally turned to Willow. She looked fresh and natural with a few freckles across her nose and her blond hair soft around her face. "What are you talking about?"

"You haven't even looked at me since last night."

He laughed, but there wasn't any humor in it. "I didn't think I wanted to broadcast to Carol my lusty thoughts."

That made Willow smile. God, he loved that smile. "So you're still lusting for me, huh?" she probed.

For you…forever. "You're a beautiful woman, Willow. I'd have to be dead not to want you again and again." This was harder to do than he realized. "But that's not in our agreement."

"Nothing is written in stone, Jack," she said as she leaned forward, her hand resting on his leg. "Who's to say we can't make a few amendments?"

Oh, yeah, and Jack knew just where to start. He took a calming breath to slow his heart rate. But sooner or later, it would end up the same for him. He'd lose. "Not a good idea."

"Why?" Willow pressed. "Because you live here, and I live in L.A.?"

"We both agreed nothing beyond last night. We have other commitments and I've been…on my own a long time. I don't do the couple thing…."

Willow stood and moved to his chair and boldly sat

down on his lap. "Maybe you haven't had the right partner." She wrapped her arms around his neck and leaned in to kiss him.

Jack groaned. She was killing him. He wanted Willow like no other woman, even allowed himself the foolish dream of having a future with her. How easy it would be to give in. Too easy. He pulled her closer and took over the kiss as his tongue slipped into her mouth to taste what he craved. Willow. And if he didn't put an end to this, it would be too late for rational thought.

He broke off the kiss, then lifted her off his lap. He stood, too. "There isn't time for this. Besides, I've already agreed to help your brother."

He didn't move a muscle as she flinched at his words.

Her anger was evident. "You think what happened between us was about Dean…?"

He shrugged. "Does it really matter? We both shared a good time…and as I understood it that's all it was supposed to be. Nothing more." He was grateful when his cell phone went off. Grabbing it off his belt, he turned away. "Sullivan."

"Mr. Sullivan, this is Ken Hastings. I have that report you wanted. I think you might be interested in what I found."

"I'll be there in thirty. Thanks, Ken."

"That was one of the Walsh network guys," he told her. "He knows who broke in and stole the money. I need to get down there."

"Can I go with you?"

The last thing he needed was her to distract him from his job. "Not a good idea. Dean and I have to be the ones who talk with Walsh."

She looked hurt, but nodded in agreement.

He didn't dare weaken on his decision. It was too easy to get lost in her…. "I'll get your brother."

Jack walked out as he punched the familiar number into his phone. Carol could come to the house and keep Willow company. He just hoped he'd have good news to bring home to her.

Two hours later, Jack and Dean stood in Stan Walsh's office. The fifty-four-year-old CEO was reading the report Ken had handed Jack when he'd arrived at Walsh Enterprises. It showed the exact times of the money transfers and identified the PC that was used. It had been traced back to Brad Lansing because of his Mac address. It even showed that he had used Dean's ID and password to gain access.

They had their thief.

Jack had already notified the police, and they picked up Lansing at his apartment, packing a suitcase with a ticket to leave the country in his possession. He was at the police station awaiting formal charges.

Walsh looked up from the report. "Brad had us all fooled." He turned to Dean. "Why didn't you come to me, son?"

Dean shrugged. "Because all fingers pointed to me and I had no way to prove my innocence. Would you have believed me over Brad?"

"Probably not. He's been with the company over three years, and I thought he'd proved his loyalty. He even showed me an idea for a security protocol he'd been developing."

"Mr. Walsh...I gave the proposal to Brad. As my supervisor, he was going to present it to you."

The man drew a tired breath. "I thought I was a pretty good judge of character."

Jack stepped in. "Stan, computer theft can happen to any company. From what the detectives got out of Lansing so far, he'd been planning this for a while. He found the perfect opportunity when Dean came to the company."

"What a mess. What am I going to tell the stockholders?"

"The truth," Jack said. "Tell them you're going to take more precautions."

Stan arched an eyebrow. "They're going to need more assurances than that."

"Then let Dean present his new protocol idea to them." Jack had worked with Dean for only hours, but he was impressed with his ideas.

Dean stepped forward. "Mr. Walsh, all I want is a chance to prove myself."

Stan studied him. "Heather's been trying to convince me how talented you are. I guess I should start listening to her." He smiled. "Why don't you come in next week and we can talk some more about your idea?" He paused. "Heather told me that you want to go home to see your mother. My daughter also told me she's invited to go along."

"She is, sir, and thank you."

"Thank Jack. He's the one who went the extra mile." The CEO looked at Jack. "Brad's in custody?"

"He's at the police station as we speak," Jack told him. "They'll need you to file criminal charges."

"Definitely. What about the million dollars?"

"The detective informed me Lansing is willing to cooperate for a reduced sentence...so there shouldn't be any problem recovering the money."

"If it weren't for the money, I wouldn't agree to let him off so easily." The older man watched Jack. "How can I thank you? You saved my company from a possible disaster."

"I was just doing what you hired me for." Jack was happy he'd found the right man.

Stan stood. "I guess you can retire your cowboy boots." He crossed the room. "If you ever change your mind and want a permanent job here, just say the word."

"Thanks, Stan, but I work better on my own." Together they walked out into the reception area. Dean was standing with the pretty redhead, Heather.

It was over. Dean was innocent. Their lives could get back to normal. Willow could go home and enjoy the summer camp. And he had no reason to go back to Wandering Creek, or to even see Willow after today.

That was the way it needed to be. A clean break, and they could move on with their lives. That was what he wanted, he told himself, over and over again.

CHAPTER NINE

WILLOW FINISHED PACKING and set her bag by the front door. She'd heard from Dean. They'd found the proof they needed. Lansing had been arrested and was at the police station.

It was over.

They could all go back to their lives, as if nothing had ever happened. But it had. Her entire life had changed. She couldn't imagine forgetting Jack. He might walk out of her life…but not her heart. She wanted it to be difficult for him to forget her, too, but that didn't look as though it was going to be the case. Not after his reminder this morning.

Her thoughts were interrupted by the sound of a knock on the back door. Willow opened it to find Carol on the stoop.

"I'm back. Thought you might need some company while you wait."

"Thanks. Please, come in. I'll share my good news with you. My brother was exonerated of any wrongdoing."

"That's wonderful." Carol grinned. "I knew if anyone could help it would be Jack."

Willow nodded as tears filled her eyes. "Now, all that's left is to fly home."

Carol didn't hesitate to embrace Willow. "Oh, sweetie, I know this has been so hard on you and your family." The older woman stroked her back. "Just cry it out."

Willow pulled herself together and stepped back. She grabbed a tissue and wiped her eyes. "I can't, Carol. If I do, I won't be able to stop. I can't let…"

Carol smiled sadly. "Jack will see how you feel about him."

She walked to the counter, but didn't look at the woman. "I've got to get through these last few hours with Jack. Oh, God, this is so hard." She paced. "I told myself I wouldn't let this happen…."

"But you fell in love with him, anyway," Carol finished for her.

All Willow could do was nod. "Don't worry…I'm not the kind of woman who hangs on to a man who doesn't want me." She raised a hand. "Jack and I made a deal…and I'm walking away."

Carol groaned. "Ooh, sometimes I want to give Jack Sean Sullivan one swift kick." The woman went to Willow. "Look, even though Mike and I were Jack's only family, we've always stayed out of his personal life. But when I saw the way he looked at you when he walked in the kitchen this morning…I was so hopeful. He's in love with you, Willow."

Willow's heart soared. "He is?"

Carol nodded slowly, deliberately. "He's never brought a woman to his home. And he called me to come and stay with you…because he was worried about you being alone."

"But he doesn't trust me, Carol. I kept something from him…."

"Jack doesn't trust many people. Too many have deserted him over the years. And he carries a lot of guilt about Mike." Carol drew a breath, then said, "He couldn't stop the shooter."

"Oh, Carol."

She shook her head. "I loved my husband, and I've come to love Jack like a son. It would have hurt if I'd lost Jack that day, too. But Jack lost Jack that day, especially after Mike's killer got off."

She couldn't believe it. "But how?"

"It was on a technicality. And the twenty-year-old boy came from a wealthy family. He was a druggie, and they hired a well-known defense attorney.

"Jack never got over it," Carol continued. "His attitude changed, and he left the force before his attitude got him in trouble. If it's any consolation, I think Jack really likes what he does. And he's good at it. But it's all he has in his life."

"He has you," Willow said.

Carol smiled. "But he needs a special someone. And I think he's found her in you. I'll see you again, I know. I think I'll head home now."

"Thanks, Carol." Willow hugged the older woman and watched her walk out. A car pulled in the drive and Dean climbed out of the backseat, followed by a pretty girl.

"Willow," he called as he went to hug her. "It's over, sis. It's really over." He rushed through the door.

"I know. I'm so happy," she cried, then pulled back. Wiping her tears, she looked over her brother's shoulder. "This must be Heather."

Dean did the introductions. "Willow, this is Heather Walsh. Heather, my sister, Willow."

"Hi, Heather. It's nice to finally meet you."

"I'm glad to meet you, too. Isn't it wonderful? Dean's been cleared of everything. And Dad's going to give him a better job."

"Security development," Dean said. "Jack told Mr. Walsh how good my idea was. Isn't that cool?"

Willow's attention went to the back door when Jack walked in. "Yeah, that's cool," she said distractedly. He was wearing khaki trousers and a light blue oxford-cloth shirt with the sleeves rolled up his forearms. She couldn't take her eyes off him, but he did everything he could to avoid her gaze.

She turned back to her brother. "Did you tell Mom?"

"Oh, no. I thought you would."

Willow grabbed her phone from her purse and dialed the ranch. There wasn't any answer at the house, so she tried the mess hall. It was answered by one of the hands, who got Molly for her.

"Oh, honey, hi," her mother said when she came on the line. "How did it go?"

She looked at Dean. "It went perfect. Dean was cleared of all charges."

"That's wonderful," she said. "We have a problem here. Curtis is missing."

"C.W.? What? When?"

"Sometime this afternoon. Can I speak to Jack?"

"Sure." She handed the phone to him. "C.W. is missing. Mom wants to talk to you."

Jack put the phone to his ear, and walked away from the group. Willow wasn't going to be shut out. She followed him.

"I knew he was angry," Jack began. "But I didn't know he'd pull this." He finally looked at Willow. "Sure, we'll be there before nightfall. Bye, Molly." He hung up and handed her back the phone.

"Damn. This is my fault."

"No, it isn't," Willow said. "C.W. ran away because that's what kids do. I've worked with neglected children for a lot of summers. They come with issues, and as much as we try, sometimes we can't help." She waved her hand. "What we need to do is find C.W."

"I'm going back." He studied her for a long time, then said, "Just until I find him. That's the only reason I'm going back to the ranch."

Willow was tired of getting these lectures. Okay, it was over between them. "Just know, Jack, C.W. has had a lot of people in and out of his life. He's grown attached to you. He's looking for…for someone to care. So don't make any promises you can't keep, especially if you're going to walk away."

Willow didn't care if she overstepped. No kid needed people to break promises.

"I know what that's like," Jack told her honestly. "I wouldn't do that to him."

She saw the pain in his eyes. She wanted to ask him more, wanted him to share his past with her. But now wasn't the time. "Okay, then we're just wasting time. Let's go back and find him."

Once they'd landed at LAX, Jack drove at record speed to the ranch. He pulled his SUV in front of the barn and climbed out followed by Dean, Heather and Willow.

They all hurried to the hall where several ranch hands were gathered outside by the sheriff's car. Inside Trevor leaned over a table, going over a map of the ranch, assigning men locations to search on horseback. Dean and Heather went to Molly, seated at another table.

"Hey, glad you're back," the foreman said and shook Jack's hand. He hugged Willow. "Sorry this happened."

"C.W. isn't the first kid to wander off over the years," Willow said. "We'll find him."

"No one has seen the boy since about two o'clock this afternoon. And we've searched everywhere in camp. The counselors have managed to keep the other kids in their routines, but they know something is going on."

Jack looked around the area, racking his brain to remember anything the kid had said that would give him a clue as to where he'd gone. "He must be working real hard trying not to be found. C.W. was angry at me for leaving. He could be hiding out."

"Hiding or not, we need to get out there and search," Willow said.

"It's going to be dark soon," Jack warned.

"So? Even in the dark, Dakota can find his way around this ranch," she said. "We can't let C.W. stay out there all night. Too many things could happen."

"Then I'm going with you," Jack said.

Willow started to argue, but knew he wasn't going to back down. "I'll have one of the hands saddle the horses while I change." She hurried off.

Jack turned back to Trevor. "Where's the boy C.W. had the fight with yesterday?"

"That would be Miguel." Trevor went to the wall and checked the list of kids' names. "Miguel Perez. He's in cabin six."

Jack took off to find the older boy's cabin. A thirteen-year-old boy came out when the counselor called him from his bunk.

The dark-haired boy stepped off the small porch. "I didn't do nothing to that kid," he began to argue.

"It's okay, Miguel," Jack said. "We just wanted to know what you fought about."

"He was bragging about how good he could ride Cisco and how he was going to be in the movie." The teenager shrugged. "I guess the guys got tired of listening to it, and called him a liar. C.W. started a fight. Joe, our counselor, broke it up and sent him to his cabin for the rest of the day.

"This morning, our group went out for a hike to the canyon and one of the guys found some gold dust at the creek. Larry told us about this old legend."

"What legend?"

The boy shrugged. "Just that there's a lost mine in the canyon that has a rich gold vein. Golden Rock."

"All the way back C.W. asked questions about the cave until the kids started teasing him. C.W. said he was going to be rich one day." The boy studied Jack. "You think the kid was crazy enough to go back there?"

"I don't know. Thanks, Miguel."

Jack met Willow as she came toward him with the horses. She handed him her father's boots. "You'll need these."

"Thanks." He sat down on the bench, toed off his shoes, then tugged the boots on. "Do you know of a place called Golden Rock Canyon?"

She blinked. "Yeah. By road it's about two miles from here. On horseback, about half that distance."

"I think that's where C.W. went. Would you believe he's looking for gold?"

After telling the sheriff their intentions, and armed with cell phones and a rifle, they rode off toward the canyon. There was about an hour of daylight left, and if they were lucky they'd find him before nightfall. But Jack didn't care either way because he wasn't going to quit until he found the boy.

The ride was fast and hard, but Willow urged Dakota on and Jack followed close behind. They were on the clock to get to C.W. before night fell, and who-knows-what came out of the wilderness. Mostly, they had one scared little boy out there. And Golden Rock wasn't the easiest place to search.

Finally they reached the edge of the canyon as the sun began its descent behind the mountains. Willow looked around the open area. Which way would he go?

"Where to?" Jack asked as he pulled up beside her.

"Not sure," she told him. "Let's follow the creek until we get to the ridge. Maybe we'll see something."

She tugged the reins and began the trek through the

shallow water as they made their way to the foothills. "If I remember right, the cave is just past a big rock. Which big rock, I'm not sure." She straightened in the saddle, trying to relieve the tension in her back.

They passed several large granite formations as they took turns calling C.W.'s name. No answer. They rode on.

"There it is." Willow pointed to the familiar formation. "I remember now. It's flat on top. C.W. It's Willow. Where are you?" she yelled.

Jack's gut churned. They had to find the boy. Darkness was falling fast as they rode up to the rock. "Where's the cave?"

"It's been years since I've been here. I think right behind there." Willow climbed off Dakota and cupped her mouth. "C.W.!"

Jack called to him, too, then listened. That was when he heard a faint sound.

Excitement rushed through him. "C.W.!"

"Jack…"

Jack scrambled up the rock formation and reached back to help Willow. They paused, holding their breath for another sound. Then it came. "That's C.W. What direction is the cave?"

Willow glanced around. "Oh, I don't know. It's been boarded up for a long time."

Jack cupped his hand to his mouth. "C.W.!"

"Jack!"

"I'm coming." Jack hurried around the rocks and in the shadows spotted a small figure.

"Curtis." He rushed to him as did Willow.

"Willow! Jack! You came back."

Seeing the dirty-faced boy was okay, Jack said, "And it looks like just in time to get you out of this mess. What happened?"

The boy's attitude returned. He gave a shrug. "I was bored."

"So you decided to go for a hike." Jack examined the tightly wedged ankle. "And go searching for gold…alone?"

C.W. looked at Willow, but she didn't help. She stood and walked away as she pulled out her cell phone and punched in a number.

"Well, Miguel was bragging about what he found."

"You still broke the rules, C.W. And if it wasn't for Miguel we wouldn't know where you went."

"I'm sorry." The boy lowered his eyes.

"You mad at me?"

Jack's chest tightened at the sadness in the boy's voice. "Any reason why I shouldn't be? You disrupted camp, and worried a lot of people. Not to mention everyone is out looking for you." He kept trying to free the boy's sneaker-covered foot.

"I'm sorry," C.W. mumbled. "I didn't mean to cause so much trouble. It's just that I got so mad…."

"At me," Jack finished for him. He drew a breath. "And I don't blame you."

"Jack," Willow interrupted him and handed C.W. a jacket for the dropping temperature. "I have the sheriff on the line. He wants to know if we need assistance."

The stubborn foot came loose. "No, I think we'll be able to bring C.W. in."

Willow spoke into the phone, then closed it. "Let's get you back to the ranch. Do you think you can stand?"

Jack helped the boy to his feet. "It hurts a little, but I think I can walk."

"Well, hang on to me just in case," Jack told him.

They made their way down the slope slowly. Jack lifted C.W. into the saddle and climbed on behind him. Willow led the way along the trail, letting Jack spend time with C.W.

"I want to apologize to you, C.W. I ran out of here pretty fast yesterday."

"It's okay."

"No, it's not. I should have explained. Willow's brother was in trouble and I wanted to help him."

The easy movement of the horse rocked them gently. "Is her brother okay?"

"Yeah, everything's okay now. Her brother's back here with his family." Jack tugged the boy's small frame against his chest.

"I'm glad Willow came back," C.W. said. "She's cool."

Jack glanced at Willow riding just ahead of them. He couldn't help but remember how she'd clung to him last night, how wonderful she made him feel. "Yeah, she's cool."

"And pretty," C.W. added. "I wish…" He paused a moment, then said, "Jack, can I tell you something? I mean…like a secret."

Jack felt humbled. "Sure. I won't tell a soul."

"I wish I had a family like Willow's," he whispered. "I mean I love my mom, but sometimes she gets…sick and can't be there for me…." C.W. stopped his words, but Jack felt the kid's hunger and longing for that make-believe family. He'd wanted the same thing so many times he'd lost count.

"Hey, how about we make a pact, C.W.?"

"About what?"

"How about if I give you my phone number so we can keep in touch? You can call me if things get too tough, or you just want to talk."

"You mean it?"

"I mean it," he repeated.

"That's cool." There was another pause. "Do you know what else would be cool? I wish you lived here so you could hang out with me sometimes. Then you'd be around to see Willow, too."

"That would be nice, but my work is in Seattle."

Jack didn't know if seeing Willow would be a good idea. Having a man drop in and out of her life wasn't fair to her. She deserved better. A man who offered her a permanent relationship. That would be the best for her, but the worst for him.

But he cared about her enough to give her up.

CHAPTER TEN

"WHAT DO YOU MEAN he can't stay?" Jack demanded.

It was after nine o'clock. The kids were finally settled in for the night and the sheriff had wrapped up his report and returned to town. All that was left was deciding what to do with C.W.

"He broke a camp rule," Willow told Jack. "He ran away and he has to go home."

Jack knew all about rules and how to break them. "It was my fault. I let him down."

Agitated, Willow marched across the empty mess hall, then back again. "A lot of people have let him down, Jack. In fact all these kids have been let down at one time or another. But this camp can't run properly by making exceptions. What if the next kid to run away gets hurt...or worse? I can't take that chance. I can't watch one kid twenty-four hours a day."

Bonnie Harris walked in. "We weren't able to reach Curtis's mother," the coordinator said. "I will have to find him a bed in foster care for the next few nights."

That tore at Jack's gut. "No, you can't do that."

Willow didn't look happy about it, either. "We don't have a choice."

"Yes, you do," he insisted. "Keep him here for the rest of the camp and I'll stay and be responsible for him."

This was the last thing Willow needed, for Jack to stay. They'd already said their goodbyes.

"What about your job?" she asked.

He shrugged. "I'm my own boss."

"So then we reward C.W. for what he did?"

"No. What C.W. did was wrong," Jack told her. "And he needs to be punished. How about he does physical work around here? Maybe clean out a few horse stalls, or doing extra kitchen work?"

Willow glanced at Bonnie, then back at Jack.

"It's only until Sunday noon," he continued. "Come on, C.W. needs the experience of camp. If only to socialize with other kids."

"And get attached to you even more," Willow said. She knew the feeling. "And then you go back to Seattle?"

"Kids get attached to a lot of people. This camp is supposed to be a good experience. Probably the best C.W. has had."

Willow looked at Bonnie, who shrugged. "It's not a problem for me, so you two work it out." She walked out, leaving them alone.

"Come on, Willow. Let me help him."

Who would help her? Help her forget the man she loved when he'd be around to remind her of what she couldn't have. The memories of last night wouldn't go away, either. Not for a long time…maybe never.

She pushed away the thoughts. "He can't take part in the movie."

"That's fair," Jack agreed. "C.W. shouldn't be able to participate. Maybe, with my help, he can do some of the grunt work behind the scenes."

"That you'll have to discuss with Mom. This is her production. I have a camp to run."

Trevor walked in. "Sorry to bother you, Willow, but there's another problem. The cook, Maggie, has a family crisis and had to leave."

Willow closed her eyes. This was one of those times she had to weigh the good against the bad. The good, they'd cleared her brother of any wrongdoing, and finding C.W. safe had topped the list. The rest she could handle. She thought of Jack. Maybe.

"Willow, I think I have a replacement." Jack pulled out his phone and walked away. Across the room, he smiled at whatever the person said to him.

A strange feeling stirred inside her. She was jealous of a phone conversation. Great. If she couldn't handle that how could she handle another four days with this man?

He returned. "I got a replacement. The new cook will be here in the morning."

"Who is it?"

"Carol," he said. "And before you ask, yes, she has experience. She helps out at a homeless shelter weekly and at her church."

Carol was coming here. Willow found she was excited about seeing her again. "Good, but she stays at the house."

Jack smiled. "She'll get a kick out of that."

"Good, it's settled. I think I'll call it a night." She

started to walk off when Jack reached for her. She felt the warmth sear her skin. She turned around.

"I know everything happened so fast we didn't get a chance to talk…."

She didn't want to do this now, maybe never. "There's nothing to talk about, Jack. Like you said, we had our night." She prayed she could hold it together. "That's all we agreed to. So if you think I was going to try and hang on…"

He came closer. "No, Willow, I just wanted to say last night was unbelievable. And if things were different…if I could be who you needed—"

She shook her head. "You have no idea what I need, Jack, or you'd never say that." She blinked rapidly at the tears. "Right now, it's best if we just concentrate on the camp. It's more than enough to keep us busy."

He nodded. "I'll try to stay out of your way." He stood there for a long time, then walked away. Willow wanted to call him back…to keep their magic going.

But she wasn't crazy enough to think she could keep a man who didn't want her.

By midmorning the next day, Jack had finished in the kitchen with C.W. He was surprised the boy liked the idea of working together.

Jack Sullivan, a big brother to a kid? It was an insane idea. He definitely was no Mike Gerick.

"Hey, Jack. Am I doing this right?"

Jack leaned over the gate as the boy mucked the horse stall. "Not bad. Make sure you get all of it."

A few minutes later they wheeled out the full barrow

to the pile behind the barn. On his return trip, Willow drove up and Carol climbed out of the ranch SUV.

Jack hugged her. "Carol, you made it."

"Yes. Willow met me at the airport." She raised an eyebrow. "We had quite a talk."

He didn't want to know what the two women discussed. He put his arm around C.W.'s shoulder and brought him closer. "Carol, this is C.W. C.W. this is Carol Gerick. She's going to help out with the cooking."

"Hello, Miss Carol." The boy stuck out his hand, but instead Carol pulled him into a big hug.

"It's good to meet you, C.W. I'm so glad you were found okay."

The kid smiled. "So am I. Now, I'm Jack's helper. It's my punishment."

They all laughed. "Well, I'm glad it all worked out."

Willow came around the car with a suitcase. "Come on, Carol, let's get you settled in." She flashed Jack a look. "These guys need to get back to work."

Jack watched the two women walk away, realizing how much they both meant to him.

"Willow's mad at you," C.W. said. "Is it because of me?"

"No, kid. It's all about me, and what I can't give her."

The boy looked up. Freckles dotted his nose and his dark blond hair needed cutting. "Maybe if you can try harder."

There was no denying he cared about Willow more than he'd thought possible. But what kind of life could he give her? Nothing like what she'd been used to. "Can I tell you a secret? I'm just plain afraid."

C.W. looked surprised, then glanced toward Willow climbing the steps to the house. "I get scared, too. But mostly when I'm by myself, I'm okay when I'm with people. Maybe Willow is scared when she's alone, too."

That thought caused an ache in his chest. Was Willow feeling alone?

They entered the house and Carol gasped as she glanced around her surroundings. "Oh, it's beautiful. But, Willow, you don't need me staying here. The camp quarters would be fine."

"No, they won't be." The voice came from the dining room as Willow's mother appeared. "You must be Carol." She smiled. "It's so good to have you here."

"And you are Molly Reynolds Kingsley. Oh, Mrs. Kingsley, I'm thrilled to meet you."

"Please, get over that. I'm just Molly." Her mother smiled. "We're going to be good friends. For one, you're special to Jack, and for another, you're saving us, agreeing to cook."

"I love to cook, and I love kids. And I get to meet a star."

"Carol was a big fan of Dad's," Willow said.

"Weren't we all," her mother said. "Matt was a wonderful man. But from what I hear, so was your Mike. We have a lot in common already. Let's go have some coffee." She took Carol's hand and started out of the room. "I also am crazy about Jack. And I think he's perfect for Willow."

"Mother!" Willow called in warning, but only got a wave of dismissal as the new best friends disappeared into the kitchen.

The last thing Willow needed was for her mother to play matchmaker. Problem was she didn't know how to stop her. She smiled. She'd let Jack deal with them. That would make him sorry he agreed to stay.

The next day of camp, things went smoothly. Carol's food was great, and the kids got back into a routine. By the second day, C.W. was off restriction and back riding Cisco. The other campers had gotten friendlier with the boy, too.

The older kids spent all their free time rehearsing for the movie scheduled to be filmed that Friday. Molly had even managed to get Carol to help out with the production, too.

In the past forty-eight hours, the two women had become like old friends. Willow had a feeling that the pair was up to something. Even Dean and Heather had gotten involved with the campers, helping out with the film. She'd also noticed that her brother had managed to spend part of his time with Jack, too.

As promised, Jack had kept his distance from her. Willow thought that would help but it hadn't. She'd lain awake at night thinking about him. Having him around was painful. It was worse to know that by Sunday he'd be gone from her life…for good.

She gripped the steering wheel of the Jeep as it climbed the trail up to Liberty. She needed to check on some equipment, so everything would be ready for the big day of filming. She'd nearly reached the town when suddenly the Jeep choked and finally died as it rolled to a stop.

She looked down at the gas gauge to see the arrow on empty. "Great," she murmured as she climbed out of the vehicle. With Liberty in her sight, she started to walk. She misjudged the rough terrain and her foot caught on a piece of root and twisted her ankle.

"Ouch," she murmured, pulling her leg up. After the pain subsided, she used the side of the Jeep and stood up and hobbled the short distance into town. It was deserted this late in the afternoon. But all she needed was the phone to have someone come and get her since she'd left her cell phone at the ranch.

On Main Street she spotted the truck. Good, someone could give her a ride back. She continued her journey on her sore ankle when Jack come out of the building.

He spotted her immediately, then ran toward her. "Willow. What happened?"

"The Jeep ran out of gas just down the hill and I twisted my ankle."

He scooped her up into his arms. "You need to get off it."

"I can walk," she argued weakly as her arms slipped around his neck. He carried her inside the saloon to the back office. "Just take me back to the ranch and I'll put some ice on it."

He ignored her and set her down on the sofa, then went for her boot. "This might hurt."

She refused to react. "I can wait until we get back."

He looked concerned. "If it starts to swell, we might have to cut off your boot."

"No. These are already broken in." She grabbed the back of the sofa. "Just do it."

She bit down on her lip as Jack tried to be gentle.

Once the boot was removed, he walked out of the room, then returned a few minutes later with a towel wrapped around some ice. He tossed his hat on the desk and sat down on the sofa. "There's all the comforts of home. The refrigerator is stocked with drinks and water. The freezer had ice."

"Bless my mother for being prepared." The cool ice was beginning to numb the pain, making her aware of Jack's hands on her. His closeness.

His dark eyes locked on hers. "Better?"

She forced a smile. As much as she tried to keep her distance from him…now here she was stranded with him. "Thank you."

"It wasn't exactly a good idea to come up here on an empty tank. What would have happened if I hadn't been here?"

She might love this man, but he infuriated her. "I would have limped to the phone. And I didn't come up here knowing I was low on gas. I'll call Trevor to come and get me."

"That's crazy, I'm here."

"Oh, I wouldn't want to put you out."

"Lady, you've put me out from the moment I laid eyes on you."

His words hurt her deeply. She couldn't even say anything. She glanced away.

"Oh, God, Willow." Jack scooted toward her. "I didn't mean it like that. I only meant…"

"What? That I'm a pain in the butt."

"No. I meant that from the first time I saw you…you took my breath away. Every time I'm close to you…you tempt me. I feel this need to touch you…." He leaned closer. "To kiss you."

"Then why…" Her words were cut off as his mouth captured hers in a hungry kiss. The heat radiated through her entire body. If this was all she could have, then she'd take it. She wrapped her arms around his neck and let him deepen the kiss. His tongue moved against hers and she whimpered in surrender.

He finally pulled back and his hand touched her cheek. "I can't think clearly whenever you're around."

"Thinking isn't always a good thing. Can't you just feel…let it happen?"

His forehead rested against hers. "I wish, but you're different, Willow. I don't want to hurt you."

Before she could argue, the phone on the desk rang. Jack got up and answered it. "She's here with me." He paused and listened, but didn't look at her. "Right, we'll be there in twenty minutes."

"Your mother was worried. We need to get back." He stuck his hat on his head. "You ready? I'll send Trevor back up to check the equipment."

Jack lifted her and carried her out to the truck. Willow knew that he wouldn't pursue her again. She had to figure out how to survive the next forty-eight hours, then let Jack walk away.

That night, Jack left the bunkhouse and walked the grounds. He found he enjoyed the quiet, the peacefulness. It was better than lying in his bunk unable to sleep…again. He hadn't slept since the night he'd spent with Willow. With her curled up in his arms, he'd slept well.

Made him think long and hard about crazy things like…hanging around…trying to come up with a way of making a life with her.

He shook his head. Nothing he'd done could stop him from thinking about her. And today's kiss nearly drove him over the edge. He knew he didn't belong in her life any more than she belonged in his.

Then why did he want her so much?

"Trouble sleeping?"

Jack turned and found Carol coming down the lighted pathway from the house. "Looks like I'm not the only one. It's a little late for you, too."

"I think we're awake for different reasons. I was visiting with Molly, and finishing up details on the filming. Had a great final rehearsal today and the costumes came out perfect."

"I heard," he said. "I took C.W. riding so he wouldn't feel he'd missed out so much."

"You're good with him." In a comfortable silence, they walked for a while, then turned back toward the main house.

"It's so nice here, Jack. Peaceful. I can see why Willow loves it so." She glanced at him. "But I bet she'd give it all up in a second if she got the right offer."

Jack had never played games with Carol and he wasn't going to start now. "That's just it, I can't offer her what she needs. I'm not that steady nine-to-five kind of guy."

Carol stopped. "Excuse me, who said life is all about those hours? Doctors, nurses, policemen, all work different hours."

"I'm talking about steady work. A job that doesn't involve living out of a car, and tailing people."

"I don't think Willow cares as much about the job as she does the man. And I happen to think you're a great catch."

God, he'd been some lucky kid to find Mike and Carol. "You're a little biased."

"You're a good man, Jack Sullivan," she told him. "I wish you could see that, too. Willow loves you the way you are. And if you were honest, you'd admit that you're in love with her, too. You do love her, don't you?"

He glanced away. "Yeah, enough to back away."

"Really?" She raised an eyebrow. "Does the thought of leaving her tear at your insides?"

He nodded. "All the way through to my gut."

"Then imagine how Willow feels right now. She loves you, too." She touched his arm. "Give it a chance, Jack. Believe me, not all people are lucky enough to find this kind of love. Grab on to it."

"It's never been about my feelings," he stressed. "We're just so different. Look around here…." He spread his arms. "I can't give her all this."

They'd reached the house, climbed the steps and Carol sat down on the porch chair. Jack took the railing.

"Last night Molly and I talked for a long time," Carol began. "I learned about her husband and their life together. Matt's poor childhood. He was even an abused child. He ran away and found his way out here to California. He built a life for himself, found a woman to love…and had a family." Her gaze met his. "I think Willow sees those same traits in you that she loved in her father." She reached out and touched his hand. "Any woman would be lucky to have you, Jack. And Willow wants you."

His heart pounded. "How can I ask her to move to Seattle? This ranch and the camp are so important to her."

"Then relocate here," she suggested. "You could expand your business. You have clients in L.A. Spread the word, Jack. You'll have more business than you can handle right here in Southern California."

Excitement raced through him, but there was still one thing he couldn't ignore. "What about you?"

Carol smiled. "It's so sweet that you worry about me, and I admit I'm selfish enough to like having you close by. But I'm making some changes, too. I decided to go live with my sister in San Diego. She's been asking me since Mike's death."

He blinked. "You've been busy," Jack said.

"I've decided that I'm too young to not think about my future. Mike wouldn't want either of us to give up on life." She smiled sadly. "It's time, Jack. It's time to stop feeling guilty that you didn't do enough for Mike. You did everything you could do as a cop…and as his friend. Now, you need to move on with your life."

Jack felt tightness circle his heart. He had hope for the first time in a long time. Could he have it all? Willow…a family… So many forgotten hopes and dreams flashed through his head.

He only prayed she'd be willing to give him another chance.

CHAPTER ELEVEN

WILLOW NEVER THOUGHT she'd be happy to see summer camp come to an end. But she only had one more day and she'd get her wish. When it was over, Jack would leave. Having him around daily had been a painful reminder that he didn't want her.

She headed Dakota toward the corral. She'd been up to Liberty, working with the kids on the movie. The film crew had finished the filming. After some editing on the high-definition video, they'd have it finished for the showing on Sunday right before the camp concluded.

A lot of things would end that day. The kids would go back to their homes. And Jack would be going to his…in Seattle.

Willow's chest ached. She knew it was time for some changes in her life, too.

Her mother was already moving on. The two-week camp just might turn into a film school. At the very least. Molly had plans to rent out Liberty for other TV and film projects. The income would help with the cost of the summer camp.

Willow needed to move on, too. Maybe she could start by moving back into L.A. She'd talked to Bonnie Harris about going to work at Fairhaven House. Of course, she wouldn't get rich, but helping kids would be something she enjoyed. With her college degree in child development, she could become a counselor at Fairhaven. Maybe she'd even go back to school.

Willow felt her throat close up with emotion. She had to do something…besides wasting time thinking about what could have been…with Jack.

She tugged on Dakota's reins as she reached the barn. Hearing her name, she turned to see C.W. running toward her. She climbed down as the boy reached her.

"Willow, I've been looking for you."

She glanced down at a drooping red rose in the boy's hand. "C.W., is something wrong?"

He worked to catch his breath. "No, but I need to give you this." He pushed the long-stemmed flower at her. "And this, too…" He presented a small envelope from behind his back. She took both, but before she could ask anything, C.W. ran off.

She looked down at the dirt-smudged card, then opened it and read…

Willow, I need to see you. Please, meet me at the bridge. J.

She didn't think she could hurt more, but she did. Then she felt the anger take over. "You've got a lot of nerve, Jack Sullivan."

"Problems?" Trevor asked.

"Just one, and I plan to deal with it." She swung up in the saddle. "Call my cell if you need me."

Trevor smiled. "Take all the time you need."

"What I have to do isn't going to take long."

Jack paced back and forth along the creek bank. Willow wasn't coming. Maybe C.W. couldn't find her. So many doubts were clouding his head when he heard the sound of horse's hooves on the wooden bridge.

He turned in time to see Willow riding toward him. He came out to greet her. "Willow…thanks for coming."

She climbed down, ignoring his help. But he knew her ankle was still sore by her slight limp. "I'm not staying long." She faced him. "How long could it take to say goodbye? Goodbye, Jack."

Jack swallowed back the dryness in his throat. "That's it. You won't even listen to what I have to say?"

She jammed her fists on her hips. "To say what? That we don't belong together. Well, I've heard it already. I don't need to hear it again. So pack your things and go." Tears flooded her eyes. "I don't want you here."

He took a chance. "What if I want to stay?"

Her rich blue gaze met his. "Don't, Jack. If you care about me at all, don't make any promises."

"Willow…" He reached for her, but she moved back, causing the horse to dance away, too. "Just listen… please." He motioned to the blanket spread under the tree and the cooler of wine placed by the trunk.

"Could we sit down for a minute and talk?"

She hesitated, then finally dropped Dakota's reins by

the creek and walked into the shade. "There isn't anything left to say."

"There's a lot, or you wouldn't have come," he said as she glared at him. He directed her to a seat on the edge of the blanket. He went to the other side. "The first is, I was wrong."

She blinked. "About what?"

"A lot of things…everything. You were right to say I was running away. And I've gotten pretty good at it when it came to relationships." When she didn't say anything, he continued, "I've decided I'm not going back to Seattle. I've decided to sell my business and move to L.A."

He enjoyed her surprised look. "Why?"

"I need a change. In fact, Dean and I have discussed working together. I convinced him that he could make a lot more money, if he was an independent contractor. So we're forming a security company. I'm handling the business end, and Dean will design and install his protocols."

She looked confused. "I thought Dean was working for Walsh Enterprises?"

"That's where he'll start. Walsh owns companies in the L.A. area. Stan wants Dean's protocols installed in their systems. You could say that his future father-in-law is Dean's first client."

"And Dean wants this, too?"

He nodded. "Your brother wants to be his own man. He's going to be in Seattle for a while, but he wouldn't mind moving closer to you and Molly. Heather wouldn't mind coming to Southern California, either. We still have several details to work out…but it looks like a go."

Willow didn't know how to react. She was numb. Her brother was returning home, but she got Jack, too. Just not how she wanted him. "I appreciate you letting me know." She started to get up. His hand went to her arm.

"That's not all I wanted to say, Willow. I didn't relocate for your brother. I'm coming to L.A. because of you. I want to be with you."

She felt her body start to tremble. His dark eyes pinned her to the spot, making her want him again. She'd be foolish to let him get to her again. She shook her head.

"Don't say that." She stood. "I can't let you in again. It hurts too much when you decide you want to leave because you're bored or restless. When I'm not enough to keep you." She blinked back tears and turned away.

"No, Willow." He moved across the blanket behind her. "You were always enough to keep me. Truth was, I didn't think I was enough for you. God, from the first you knocked me right off my feet."

She couldn't turn around or she'd be lost. Lost in his eyes, in his voice…in his arms.

But he didn't stop trying to break down her resistance. "That first day when I saw you out riding Dakota," he whispered in her ear, "you were so beautiful. And then your temper kicked in, and that fierce protectiveness of your friends and family. It's a powerful combination for a man who ached to have what you had, but never thought he could."

She couldn't stop herself and turned to see his smile. "You caused feelings in me, Willow, feelings I never knew could exist between two people. It was nothing I'd ever experienced with another woman. Only with you."

"Jack…don't do this."

He raised a hand. "I'm going to do everything I need to do to get you. I'm going to start with honesty. I didn't have a good childhood. I did things to survive, things I'm not proud of." He swallowed hard. "Mike was my salvation. When he died, I wanted to die, too. And when the kid who took my best friend from me got off, I wanted to hunt him down and kill him myself." His watery dark eyes met hers and she reached out to touch his cheek.

"Carol helped me, and I got counseling, but I still walked through life…just existing…." He covered her hand with his. "Then I found you. Oh, Willow…you were like fresh air breathed into me. You make me want to think about the future again. One with you."

He leaned in to kiss her, but Willow stopped him and quickly stood. She knew that if she gave in to his kisses that she'd weaken. She had to be strong.

"Willow…"

She shook her head. "I don't want to do this again, Jack. I've been with a man who said he wanted me."

"I know you were hurt, and I contributed to your pain. And I'm sorry for that. I'll do anything to make it up to you."

He'd said a lot of sweet words, but none mentioned those three special ones that Willow needed to hear. "It's all right, Jack. I forgive you," she told him, then started toward Dakota.

"No, Willow. Wait. At least give us a chance."

She blinked at her threatening tears, praying they wouldn't fall. "It wouldn't work Jack, we'd end up hurting each other," she called over her shoulder.

He followed after her, then reached for her and turned her to face him. "I'm not letting you go, Willow. If I have to I'll kidnap you until you realize how much I love you…and that we were meant to be together."

She froze at his declaration. "What did you say?"

He looked confused. "I said I'm going to kidnap—"

"No. No, after that." She couldn't stop her tears. "Tell me, Jack."

His dark gaze locked with hers as he drew her into his arms. "I love you, Willow Kingsley," he breathed. "I love you. I love you."

He lowered his head and kissed her with such tenderness. And by the time he broke off, they were both breathing hard. "I love you…" he repeated again.

"Oh, Jack," she cried as a tear rolled down her cheek. "I love you, too." Her shaky hands touched his face. "I never thought you felt—"

Jack cut off her words as he covered her mouth in another kiss. He picked her up and carried her back to the blanket as the kiss deepened and the only thing that mattered was the two of them.

Jack pulled away first and she whimpered in disappointment. "Hold that thought," he told her and quickly got on one knee. "Willow. I never thought I'd find someone like you. And today, I offer you my heart…and my love forever." He swallowed as he reached into his pocket and pulled out a ring. It was an oval-cut sapphire surrounded by diamonds glistening back at her. "Will you marry me?"

Willow was suddenly giddy. "Oh, Jack, it's beautiful." Her eyes raised to meet his. "Yes, I'll marry you."

He slipped the ring on her finger and she went back into his arms. She clung to him, feeling her love for this man about to burst from her. "Yes, I'll be your wife…your family. Always."

He grinned. "That's what I was hoping you'd say."

He kissed her again and all their problems began to slowly fade away. All that mattered was they loved each other. And that they were going to spend their lives together…forever.

EPILOGUE

SUNDAY AFTERNOON, Willow stood in the back of the assembly hall as applause broke out when the credits appeared on the movie screen. The first Kingsley Kids video, *The Legend of Liberty's Lawman*, was a success.

Molly stepped up to the podium. "There are so many people to thank for today. All the volunteers, the technical people who gave their time. If it wasn't for them, this incredible endeavor would never have taken place. There wouldn't be a movie." She glanced around at the children seated at the tables.

"And you kids. You have so much talent I can't wait to see what we accomplish next summer. As you know, I'll be looking for original scripts as our project for next year, so pass the word around." She drew a breath. "There's more news. We'll be putting together a program for high school students interested in working in the film industry. We've named it MATTS School. MATTS stands for Movie Apprenticeship for Technically Talented Students.

"It's also named after my late husband. He loved this camp and the kids." Molly glanced around, unashamed of the tears in her voice. "I think he'd be so happy that we used his town, Liberty, as our first project."

Cheers and applause broke out again, and they began to chant Molly's name. She raised her hand to quiet the crowd. "It's tough to say goodbye, so we'll say so long—until next year."

After dismissal, several of the students went to the front and hugged Molly, while others headed for the buses.

Willow smiled. It had been a crazy summer to say the least, but in the end it had worked out so…perfect for everyone.

At the van she saw Jack standing with C.W. She glanced down at her engagement ring. Perfect.

Jack had known this would be difficult, but he'd never planned on feeling like this. "I promise, C.W., I'll see you next weekend."

The boy nodded. "Okay. But if you can't be there I'll know you're busy."

Jack finally knelt down in front of him. "Look, C.W., I'm not going to desert you. I've talked with your mother, and I've signed up for the Big Brother program at Fairhaven, so you're stuck with me. You better get used to it."

He still wasn't convinced. "What about Willow?"

"What about her? You like her, don't you?"

"Yeah, she's cool. But you're gonna want to be with her a lot. I mean, you're marrying her."

"I am, but I want to spend time with you, too." Jack knew how insecure the kid felt. So many people had let him down. "Who else wants to look at my baseball card collection, or see pictures of my days as a cop?"

"You really gonna bring them?"

Jack nodded. It had been Willow who'd made him realize that he should celebrate the time he had had with Mike and their years together on the force.

"Make him show you his medals, too."

Hearing Willow's voice, they turned as she came up to them.

C.W.'s eyes widened. "You have medals? Wow!"

Jack smiled at the woman he loved more than life. "Yeah, but no one was supposed to know about them."

Willow wiggled an eyebrow. "A little birdie told me."

He knew it had to be Carol. "If I can find them," he told the boy, "I'll bring them down, too."

Willow walked up to C.W. "I'll help him look."

The counselors called out to load up.

Willow bent down and hugged C.W. "Hope to see you soon, C.W. Bye." She stepped back, giving the guys their time.

"So next weekend we go to the movies. You pick which one."

C.W. nodded, then suddenly the boy launched himself into Jack's arms. He grabbed the kid in a tight embrace. Funny thing, it was Jack who seemed to need the contact more than C.W. There was something else he felt. Mike. Mike was there with him.

What goes around comes around, kid. You did good, Jack, my boy.

Emotion welled in Jack as he managed to release C.W. and guide him to the van. Willow stepped into his arms as they waved to the kids one last time. The dust kicked up on the road as the chain of vans headed to the highway.

Willow looked at him. "You okay?"

He nodded. "I felt Mike. It was as if he was right here."

Willow hugged him a little tighter. "I know the feeling. I felt my dad was here during the movie."

Jack had to swallow before he could get the words out. "Mike said I did good."

She looked up at him. He'd never tire of the look of love in her eyes.

"I hope you believe him," she said. "You've changed C.W.'s life. He's a lucky little boy to have you. And I'm a lucky big girl to have you, too." She raised up and placed a kiss on his lips.

"I'm the lucky one," Jack countered. "When are you going to marry me? I'm not crazy about sleeping in the bunkhouse."

Willow smiled. "I think you'll have to consult with the mothers." She nodded toward Molly and Carol. "They're in charge of the big day."

Jack turned her in his arms. "Just so long as I'm in charge of the honeymoon." He captured her mouth in a searing kiss that left them both a little breathless.

"Oh, my—I think I'm going to like you being in charge."

"You say that now, but I'm marrying a woman with her own mind. I think we'll tangle many times in our future together." He loved the sound of that. Their future.

She pressed against him. "Oh, but think about how much fun it'll be to make up."

"Yeah, there is that," he said, feeling his need for her intensify.

They'd decided to wait until October to be married, giving everyone time to recoup from camp. And until Jack sold his home in Seattle they planned to live here at the ranch. Then eventually they would buy a place just outside of L.A., or build a home right there at Wandering Creek.

Jack knew he didn't plan to travel much. He had enough to keep him busy in Southern California, and someone to come home to every night.

Willow had already gotten a job at Fairhaven House. Though she was only going to volunteer. They'd decided not to wait long to start on a family. Just the thought shot desire through him.

"How about we find a little privacy now?" He glanced around at all the people still mingling around. "How about a ride to our special place?"

The cover bridge. It was where they'd found each other. Where they had declared their love…their commitment to one another.

"Sure, I'll have the horses saddled."

"I was thinking of another kind of horse to ride." He pulled out the key to her Mustang.

"Oh, Jack. My car, it's fixed?"

He nodded. "It was delivered this morning. With camp breaking up, it was too hectic to tell you." They started walking toward the house and garage area. There in the drive was parked her shiny red '66 Mustang.

She hurried to do a closer examination. "She's beautiful."

"Want to go for a drive?" he asked.

She nodded. "It's a perfect day for it," she said, walking around to the passenger side. "You drive." Willow tossed him the key and climbed in. "It's just like in the movies," she said, smiling. "I get to ride off into the sunset with my guy."

Jack felt the thrill as he sat behind the wheel. "And the guy gets the girl…forever."

"Oh, I love happy endings."

He reached over and kissed her tenderly. "It's only the beginning, Willow. Only the beginning."

* * * * *

Look for LAST WOLF WATCHING
by Rhyannon Byrd—the exciting conclusion in the
BLOODRUNNERS *miniseries*
from Silhouette Nocturne.

Follow Michaela and Brody on their fierce journey to
find the truth and face the demons from the past, as
they reach the heart of the battle between the Runners
and the rogues.

Here is a sneak preview of book three,
LAST WOLF WATCHING.

Michaela squinted, struggling to see through the impenetrable darkness. Everyone looked toward the Elders, but she knew Brody Carter still watched her. Michaela could feel the power of his gaze. Its heat. Its strength. And something that felt strangely like anger, though he had no reason to have any emotion toward her. Strangers from different worlds, brought together beneath the heavy silver moon on a night made for hell itself. That was their only connection.

The second she finished that thought, she knew it was a lie. But she couldn't deal with it now. Not tonight. Not when her whole world balanced on the edge of destruction.

Willing her backbone to keep her upright, Michaela Doucet focused on the towering blaze of a roaring bonfire that rose from the far side of the clearing, its orange flames burning with maniacal zeal against the inky black curtain of the night. Many of the Lycans had already shifted into their preternatural shapes, their fur-covered bodies standing like monstrous shadows at the

edges of the forest as they waited with restless ex-
pectancy for her brother.

Her nineteen-year-old brother, Max, had been
attacked by a rogue werewolf—a Lycan who preyed
upon humans for food. Max had been bitten in the attack,
which meant he was no longer human, but a breed of
creature that existed between the two worlds of man and
beast, much like the Bloodrunners themselves.

The Elders parted, and two hulking shapes emerged
from the trees. In their wolf forms, the Lycans stood
over seven feet tall, their legs bent at an odd angle as
they stalked forward. They each held a thick chain that
had been wound around their inside wrists, the twin
lengths leading back into the shadows. The Lycans had
taken no more than a few steps when they jerked on the
chains, and her brother appeared.

Bound like an animal.

Biting at her trembling lower lip, she glanced left, then
right, surprised to see that others had joined her. Now the
Bloodrunners and their family and friends stood as a
united force against the Silvercrest pack, which had yet
to accept the fact that something sinister was eating away
at its foundation—something that would rip down the
protective walls that separated their world from the
humans'. It occurred to Michaela that loyalties were
being announced tonight—a separation made between
those who would stand with the Runners in their fight
against the rogues and those who blindly supported the
pack's refusal to face reality. But all she could focus on
was her brother. Max looked so hurt…so terrified.

"Leave him alone," she screamed, her soft-soled,

black satin slip-ons struggling for purchase in the damp earth as she rushed toward Max, only to find herself lifted off the ground when a hard, heavily muscled arm clamped around her waist from behind, pulling her clear off her feet. "Damn it, let me down!" she snarled, unable to take her eyes off her brother as the golden-eyed Lycan kicked him.

Mindless with heartache and rage, Michaela clawed at the arm holding her, kicking her heels against whatever part of her captor's legs she could reach. "Stop it," a deep, husky voice grunted in her ear. "You're not helping him by losing it. I give you my word he'll survive the ceremony, but you have to keep it together."

"Nooooo!" she screamed, too hysterical to listen to reason. "You're monsters! All of you! Look what you've done to him! How dare you! *How dare you!*"

The arm tightened with a powerful flex of muscle, cinching her waist. Her breath sucked in on a sharp, wailing gasp.

"Shut up before you get both yourself and your brother killed. I will *not* let that happen. Do you understand me?" her captor growled, shaking her so hard that her teeth clicked together. "Do you understand me, Doucet?"

"Damn it," she cried, stricken as she watched one of the guards grab Max by his hair. Around them Lycans huffed and growled as they watched the spectacle, while others outright howled for the show to begin.

"That's enough!" the voice seethed in her ear. "They'll tear you apart before you even reach him, and I'll be damned if I'm going to stand here and watch you die."

Suddenly, through the haze of fear and agony and

outrage in her mind, she finally recognized who'd caught her. *Brody.*

He held her in his arms, her body locked against his powerful form, her back to the burning heat of his chest. A low, keening sound of anguish tore through her, and her head dropped forward as hoarse sobs of pain ripped from her throat. "Let me go. I have to help him. *Please*," she begged brokenly, knowing only that she needed to get to Max. "Let me go, Brody."

He muttered something against her hair, his breath warm against her scalp, and Michaela could have sworn it was a single word…. But she must have heard wrong. She was too upset. Too furious. Too terrified. She must be out of her mind.

Because it sounded as if he'd quietly snarled the word *never*.

nocturne™

THE FINAL INSTALLMENT OF THE BLOODRUNNERS TRILOGY

Last Wolf Watching

Runner Brody Carter has found his match in
Michaela Doucet, a human with unusual psychic powers.
When Michaela's brother is threatened, Brody becomes
her protector, and suddenly not only has to protect her
from her enemies but also from himself....

LOOK FOR

LAST WOLF WATCHING
BY
RHYANNON BYRD

Available May 2008 wherever you buy books.

Dramatic and Sensual Tales of Paranormal Romance

www.eHarlequin.com   SN61786

Jason Welborn was convinced that his business partner's daughter, Jenny, had come to claim her share in the business. But Jenny seemed determined to win him over, and the more he tried to push her away, the more feisty Jenny's response. Slowly but surely she was starting to get under Jason's skin....

Look for

Coming Home to the Cattleman

by

JUDY CHRISTENBERRY

Available May wherever you buy books.

www.eHarlequin.com

HRI7511

SPECIAL EDITION™

 THE WILDER FAMILY
Healing Hearts in Walnut River

Social worker Isobel Suarez was proud to
work at Walnut River General Hospital, so
when Neil Kane showed up from the attorney
general's office to investigate insurance fraud,
she was up in arms. Until she melted in his
arms, and things got very tricky...

Look for

HER MR. RIGHT?

by

KAREN ROSE SMITH

Available May wherever books are sold.

REQUEST YOUR FREE BOOKS!
2 FREE NOVELS PLUS 2
FREE GIFTS!

HARLEQUIN ROMANCE®

From the Heart, For the Heart

YES! Please send me 2 FREE Harlequin Romance® novels and my 2 FREE gifts (gifts are worth about $10). After receiving them, if I don't wish to receive any more books, I can return the shipping statement marked "cancel." If I don't cancel, I will receive 4 brand-new novels every month and be billed just $3.32 per book in the U.S. or $3.80 per book in Canada, plus 25¢ shipping and handling per book and applicable taxes, if any*. That's a savings of over 15% off the cover price! I understand that accepting the 2 free books and gifts places me under no obligation to buy anything. I can always return a shipment and cancel at any time. Even if I never buy another book, the two free books and gifts are mine to keep forever.

114 HDN ERQW 314 HDN ERQ9

Name _____ (PLEASE PRINT) _____

Address _____ Apt. # _____

City _____ State/Prov. _____ Zip/Postal Code _____

Signature (if under 18, a parent or guardian must sign)

Mail to the **Harlequin Reader Service:**
IN U.S.A.: P.O. Box 1867, Buffalo, NY 14240-1867
IN CANADA: P.O. Box 609, Fort Erie, Ontario L2A 5X3

Not valid to current subscribers of Harlequin Romance books.

Want to try two free books from another line?
Call 1-800-873-8635 or visit www.morefreebooks.com.

* Terms and prices subject to change without notice. N.Y. residents add applicable sales tax. Canadian residents will be charged applicable provincial taxes and GST. This offer is limited to one order per household. All orders subject to approval. Credit or debit balances in a customer's account(s) may be offset by any other outstanding balance owed by or to the customer. Please allow 4 to 6 weeks for delivery. Offer available while quantities last.

Your Privacy: Harlequin Books is committed to protecting your privacy. Our Privacy Policy is available online at www.eHarlequin.com or upon request from the Reader Service. From time to time we make our lists of customers available to reputable third parties who may have a product or service of interest to you. If you would prefer we not share your name and address, please check here. ☐

HR08

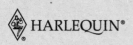

HARLEQUIN®

American ★ Romance®

Three Boys and a Baby

When Ella Garvey's eight-year-old twins and
their best friend, Dillon, discover an abandoned
baby girl, they fear she will be put in jail—
or worse! They decide to take matters into their
own hands and run away. Luckily the outlaws are
found quickly…and Ella finds a second chance
at love—with Dillon's dad, Jackson.

LOOK FOR

Three Boys and a Baby

BY

LAURA MARIE ALTOM

*Available May
wherever you buy books.*

LOVE, HOME & HAPPINESS

www.eHarlequin.com   HAR75215

Coming Next Month

It's raining men this month at Harlequin Romance®, with a rancher,
an Italian playboy, a sheikh boss, a Boston society heir, an
entrepreneur to the rescue and a single dad to melt your heart!

#4021 COMING HOME TO THE CATTLEMAN Judy Christenberry
Western Weddings

What does home mean to you? For Jenny, it's a distant memory. But this
time going home brings her into conflict with the aloof and brooding Jason,
her dad's business partner, who has been less than welcoming....

#4022 THE ITALIAN PLAYBOY'S SECRET SON Rebecca Winters
Mediterranean Dads

In the second book of the spectacular duet, a terrifying crash has put race
car driver Cesar Villon de Falcon in hospital, fighting for his life. Sarah has
come to tell him a secret that will bring him back to life: he has a son!

#4023 THE HEIR'S CONVENIENT WIFE Myrna Mackenzie
The Wedding Planners

The series continues with more bridal fun! Photographer Regina realizes
she hardly knows the man she conveniently wed. He may be strong,
honorable and the heir to Boston's most distinguished business empire...
but what about the man inside?

#4024 HER SHEIKH BOSS Carol Grace
Desert Brides

Duty is the most important thing in Sheikh Samir's life—an arranged
marriage to a suitable woman was always his destiny. But then, on a
business trip in the desert, Samir starts to see his sensible but spirited
assistant Claudia in a whole new light....

#4025 WANTED: WHITE WEDDING Natasha Oakley

Do you dream of the perfect white wedding? Freya spent hours planning
hers when she was young as a way to escape the troubles of home. Now
she's made something of her life and all that's missing is someone to
share it with—until she meets a gorgeous single dad....

#4026 HIS PREGNANT HOUSEKEEPER Caroline Anderson
Baby on Board

Wealthy architect Daniel can't turn his back on pregnant Iona, whom
he finds penniless and alone in a building he is redeveloping. It's all her
Cinderella fantasies come true when Daniel promises to take care of her.
But can the fairy tale really last?

HRCNM0408